# Fall From Grace

Jennifer Ballard

Copyright © 2019 Jennifer Ballard

All rights reserved.

ISBN: 9781798559864

# A Sense of Justice

My horse Sydney and I had just finished a great round in the amateur division when we were accosted by Darby Kirst, who was in the middle of one of her fits. I recognized her immediately, but I was sure she didn't know who I was.

She was wearing one of her expensive, top-quality riding outfits, trying to look like an experienced, knowledgeable horse person.

"Chuck, I swear that is my horse," she said to her companion, and then pointed at me. "You, get off my horse. Give Syndicate to me."

Sydney and I looked at her without moving, although I almost smirked at her being with someone called Chuck. The Darby I knew would have called him something dignified, like Charles, whether that was his name or not.

"Chuck, get that person off my horse!" Darby demanded.

Chuck didn't know how to handle Darby. He said, "If you think that's your horse, perhaps we should speak to the police."

Chuck looked to me like he couldn't have managed anything outside of polite, social situations.

"Since you're not going to do anything, it looks like I'll have to," she said.

She gave me one more chance. "Give me that horse right now, or I'm going to go to the police."

"I'm sorry," I said. "I don't believe this is your horse."

Darby abruptly walked away in search of a police squad, with Chuck trailing after her. I didn't know where she would find an officer of the law at a horseshow, but I figured she could get one as easily as she acquired everything else in life.

I hopped down off Sydney and walked him over to the warm up arena to watch Jaye.

"You and Sydney were great, Skip," Jaye said as soon as she saw me. "I need your help. Cinema's class is coming up and he's not getting his lead changes. Can you school him?"

"Sure. Cool Syd for me."

We traded horses. Sydney and Cinema are a lot alike. They are big, matching dark bays, with lots of white on their legs and faces. Sydney is a Thoroughbred and Cinema is a cross – something odd, like Quarter Horse and Standardbred. Being his owner, I think Sydney is more talented.

Jaye walked Sydney outside the ring, watching me work with her horse. It took a few minutes, but I finally got Cinema relaxed enough to listen to me. Sydney and I had no more classes to ride in, so when Sydney was cooled off, Jaye led him back toward the trailer.

When Cinema was finally changing his lead on cue, Darby reappeared with Chuck and two men wearing security uniforms.

"He's got a tattoo," Darby said. "He raced when he was young. I'll recognize the number. Look under his upper lip."

One of the security guys looked as puzzled as Chuck, but the other knew enough about horses to understand that all Thoroughbred horses that had ever raced on the track were marked with a tattoo. He looked comfortable around horses, not intimidated by the idea of dealing with one up close. I dismounted as he approached me and introduced myself. His name tag said "Linn".

"Would you mind if I had a look at your horses tattoo?" he asked.

"This horse doesn't have a tattoo," I said. "He's not a Thoroughbred."

The man glanced back at Darby.

"I know that is my horse!" she said. "Check the tattoo. The tattoo will prove it."

I raised Cinema's upper lip. The lack of a tattoo, or any sign of there having been one, sent Darby into another small fit.

Keeping his voice low, the security guy asked me, "Do you know anything about this woman or her stolen horse?"

I remembered hearing Darby talking to a friend at my grandfather's stable where they kept their horses. The friend had been thrown by her horse and broken three of her fingers.

"If that happened to me," Darby had said. "I would have the animal shot."

"Her horse is dead," I told Linn. "There's a record of it somewhere. She kept him at a farm where I worked. A gunshot from a neighboring farm spooked her horse and he threw her and broke her arm. She ordered the horse to be destroyed."

"I can believe that," the officer said. "I don't suppose it would do any good to remind her about it."

"Probably not."

He shook his head and went back to deal with Darby.

My grandfather had rebelled at the idea of putting Syndicate down, but he was a vet and Syndicate was Darby's horse, to do with as she liked. Syndicate was a wonderful, talented horse, easy-going enough to keep his good attitude through Darby's episodes of temper and abuse. He never should have belonged to someone like Darby.

I hadn't expected to see Darby Kirst again. I had also never really expected a close shot from my rifle to spook her horse enough to throw her.

Jaye returned after unsaddling Syd and leaving him comfortably settled near the trailer. I helped her up on Cinema and watched her ride into the ring.

I never forgot the look on my grandfather's face when he signed the papers saying that Syndicate had been destroyed. It was more than fraud; it was horse-theft. Grand larceny, or whatever they called such things in the case of a horse of Syndicate's worth.

I pointed out to Granddad that Darby didn't deserve a horse like Syndicate. And now he was mine.

# Fall From Grace

Angie's horse, Donovan, shied violently as he cantered around the corner of the arena, leaping sideways and almost dumping her on the ground.

She was riding alone out in the ring behind the barn, where Reyna had been killed a week previously. The crime scene tape had only been removed the day before. The bright yellow tape had unnerved the horses as well as the riders, for different reasons.

Reyna had been shot while out in the arena alone, practicing for an upcoming show. Angie glared at the tree lined creek on the far side of the pasture next to the small ring; the place where the shot was thought to have come from. She thought she saw a flash of something metallic in the trees glinting in the sun. Feeling as spooked as her horse, she dismounted quickly and led him back into the barn.

Kim and Carol were talking in the barn aisle.

"Angie, you're pale. Did you fall?"

"No. Almost, but I'm alright," Angie said. "Donavan spooked in that corner again and I thought…it just made me nervous."

"Everyone's kind of nervous," Kim said. "It's scary to have a killer running loose around the stable."

From having gone to college with her and years of working in the same office and riding together on weekends, Angie was used to Kim's dramatics. Carol, in her mid-thirties, liked to act as if being a decade older made her wise, or at least more sensible.

"There's not a killer running loose," Carol said. She rolled her eyes at Kim. "The shooting was an accident."

"I wouldn't bet on it," Kim said. "That's not what the police think."

Kim went into the tack room and emerged with her horse's saddle and bridle.

"What do the police think?" Carol asked. "And how do you know?"

"I heard Pete talking to the grooms. He said the police think it was a stray shot from some hunters in the woods on the other side of the creek."

"That's an accident; that's not murder," Carol argued.

"Sure it is. It's accidental murder – involuntary manslaughter or something. Those woods are part of the stable property and no one is supposed to hunt there. If Mr. Hansen allowed someone to hunt and they killed Reyna, then, as the property owner, he's responsible."

"That's not really murder, though. Not premeditated."

"If Hansen allowed hunters, he would know who it was and they would be caught," Angie said. "And Corey said they think it might have really been murder. That someone killed Reyna deliberately."

"When did you talk to Corey?" Carol asked.

"And why hasn't he been her?" Kim demanded. "Did he forget he works here? A farm this big can't function when one of the head staff members just stops showing up."

"How is he doing?" Carol asked Angie, gently. "I'm sure this has been hard for him."

"I spoke to him on the phone yesterday," Angie said. "He has been pretty torn up about this. He and Reyna only got along marginally well, but they did have a close working relationship. The police were asking him a lot of questions because Reyna was riding Corey's horse when she was shot."

"I wonder if Pete knows that," Kim said, as she spotted Pete passing by outside the open barn door. "Maybe he can give us an update."

When Kim called to him, Pete entered the barn and walked over. As manager of the farm, Pete treated every stable patron as if they were the most important. He also liked to know everything that was going on and would know a lot about the situation. Probably more than the detectives wanted anyone to know.

"Has anything new been found out about Reyna's death?" Carol asked, not trusting Kim to be phrase the question politely.

Pete considered carefully before sharing any of his information and then spoke directly to Carol. Angie and Kim didn't mind. It was no secret between them that Carol had a thing for Pete. Angie thought it was only because he took his job so seriously and he would never get involved with a client that he didn't pursue Carol. No one believed the things Reyna had said about her and Pete having a relationship, but Reyna hadn't been shy about letting everyone know about her own attraction to Pete.

"The shot was from a .22," Pete said. "That's a type of rifle, common among small game hunters, and it was fired from the woods across the pasture from the ring. It's possible it was an accident or that Reyna was killed by someone for a reason. Something having to do with the upcoming show or the horse she was riding."

"Grace?" Angie asked. "Corey's horse? How is Grace involved?"

Corey's gelding, Grace Under Pressure, was known as 'Grace' around the barn. Corey said that when Grace was younger he was called Guppy, but as he became a successful show horse, Corey decided he needed a more dignified name. Not that Grace was a particularly dignified name for a male horse, Angie thought.

"When the police looked into it, it turned out that Grace doesn't really belong to Corey," Pete said.

"Corey stole him?" Kim's enthusiasm at the possibility of intrigue temporarily overshadowed the fact that Corey was someone they—particularly Angie—cared about.

"Apparently, the horse belonged to Corey's Uncle Troy and was promised to Corey. When Troy died unexpectedly, one of Corey's cousins, Martin Stanley, took over the family farm and planned to sell the horse. So Corey took the horse and traveled across the country to come work here."

"So he did steal him," Angie said.

Pete shook his head and put a hand on Angie's shoulder.

"No need to fret," he said. "When the cops talked to Martin Stanley, Stanley said he wasn't pressing charges because the horse really should have been Corey's. He's arranged to have the papers put in Corey's name."

"So Corey's not in trouble with the law?"

"Not at all," Pete said. "I understand you two are good friends."

"Yes."

Angie didn't know if her relationship with Corey was anything more that friendship, but they spent a lot of time together and she really liked him.

"Did he ever talk to you about the horse or his uncle?" Pete asked.

"He talks about his uncle Troy all the time. They were very close. Everything his uncle gave him is very special to Corey; his car, his St. Francis medallion and especially Grace."

"You suggested Reyna's death might have something to do with the upcoming show," Carol said. "Did you mean someone might have killed Reyna to keep her from competing?"

Pete nodded.

"So people like Dale Turner and Tony Mackey, who were going to compete against her, are possible suspects?"

Pete nodded again.

"Dale and Tony?" Kim asked. "That can't be. Tony and Reyna were friends. Dale is Reyna's stepfather. The three of them have been training for this show together for weeks."

"It's no secret that Dale and Reyna hated each other," Pete pointed out. "All of us have heard Dale say that his relationship with Reyna's mother would be wonderful if Reyna ceased to exist. Dale and Reyna competing against each other didn't help things in the least."

"What are the other possibilities?" Angie asked.

"The main theory is that she was killed accidentally by someone hunting. Mr. Hansen did allow some friends to hunt on the grounds that day. However, they said they were off behind the hill and that story seems to check out."

"How could Hansen do that?" Carol said. "That is so irresponsible and stupid!"

Pete didn't say anything against his employer, but he didn't disagree with Carol's statement.

Angie wondered how Pete knew all this and why he was so willing to share it with them. He could be trying to help find out who was responsible, if only to keep his boss, Hansen out of trouble.

Maybe Pete and Reyna were as close as Reyna had always implied. Pete was businesslike—as always—so it was hard to tell if he was hurting over here death. It was possible he knew something about Reyna that might be significant.

"Could this have something to do with Reyna's writing?" Kim asked no one in particular.

Everyone looked at her.

"She was a freelance journalist," Kim said. "A couple of weeks ago she asked me something about local crime and said she was writing an article about it. Writing about crime, especially where you live sounds pretty dangerous to me."

Pete frowned thoughtfully. "I don't know if anyone's considered that. It might be worth mentioning to the detectives."

Pete left the barn and Kim and Carol continued saddling their horses. Angie stood in the barn aisle staring after Pete. He was an easy person to like, but hard to know.

"Angie," Kim called loudly. "Not taking an interest in Pete are you?"

"Too old," Angie said. "He's at least Carol's age."

"I heard that," Carol said from inside the tack room.

Angie moved closer to where Kim was waiting impatiently for Carol to finish getting ready.

"What kind of crime was Reyna talking to you about?" Angie asked.

Kim didn't bother to keep her voice down. "Stealing, embezzlement and smuggling—like what's supposedly been happening at the company Carol works for."

Carol finished putting her horse's bridle on and pulled on her gloves. "We're going to ride over the hill to the pond. Do you want to ride with us?"

"No, thanks," Angie said. "I'm doing to clean Donovan's bridle and head home."

Left alone in the barn, Angie found herself feeling deserted and scared again. She untacked and brushed her horse, returned him to his pasture and tried to concentrate on cleaning her bridle. She missed Corey's friendly and cheerful presence.

Angie was ready to leave, but was uneasy about walking to her car. Donovan was kept in the lower barn, which was the older of the two on the property and the farthest from the parking area. A newer barn, with a lounge next to the barn office, had been built and an indoor arena was built between them, connecting the two buildings.

There were various grooms and barn help around, but they were scattered and not likely to be near if she needed them. Angie had no idea why a killer would want to hurt her, but if Reyna's death was murder, no one yet knew the reason for it.

Instead of taking one of the neatly kept paths around the outside of the whole structure, she decided to cut through the barns and across the indoor arena. She found Tony and Dale standing with their horses in middle of the indoor arena. They were talking quietly, but both looked relaxed.

She didn't know either of them well. Their expensive horses were stabled in the larger barn, which cost much more for boarding. They traveled to the bigger shows, while she and Donavan competed at small local shows.

Angie found it hard to believe that anyone would kill to keep a person from competing against them. They were all amateur riders, not professional. Tony and Dale both had successful careers and appeared to be wealthy. She couldn't remember what Dale did, but Tony was some kind of executive in the company Carol worked for.

As she crossed the arena, Angie was naturally drawn to the horses, admiring their beautiful coats and markings.

"Can we help you with something?" Tony asked.

"Sorry. I'm a little nervous about being here and felt safer cutting through the barns and the ring than wandering around outside by myself," Angie said.

Dale's gelding put his ears back as Angie approached and Dale gave her a hard look. Angie stepped away from Dale and his horse, which put her closer to Tony. That wasn't much better. Tony was really tall and broad, but his expression wasn't unfriendly. He looked concerned and up close he looked much younger than she had thought.

Angie studied the two horses, thinking it was possible to tell a lot about a person from their animals. Dale's gelding, No Faults, had a personality much like his owner's—arrogant and temperamental. Tony's mare, Terza Rima was enormous, but very sweet.

"Is it the shooting that's got you spooked?" Tony shook his head. "There's no need to worry about it. Just a freak accident, the fault of that fool, Hansen."

"Probably not," Dale argued. "I think the police ought to look closer at that cousin of the groom who stole the horse. He might have tried to kill the boy to get the horse back and shot the wrong person."

The implications of Dale's words distracted Angie from admiring the horses. If the killer had meant to shoot Corey, they didn't achieve their goal, and they might try again. The fact that they might have been careless enough to shoot the wrong person the first time meant more danger for everyone.

That gave Angie another horrible idea. She said, "If they were trying to keep Reyna from competing, it could be they meant to shoot the horse."

People could be horrible to each other, but hurting defenseless animals because of human disagreements or greed seemed worse. The idea appalled her and she hadn't meant to say it out loud.

The cold looks she received from both Tony and Dale made it clear she shouldn't have said it. It pointed to them as potential suspects.

"Did someone suggest that theory?" Tony asked, keeping his voice low.

They were both staring at her, waiting for her answer.

"No, it just occurred to me now," Angie said.

"Probably not wise to go around making random observations like that," Dale said. His voice was soft and chilling.

"You're right," Angie said, suddenly wishing she were completely alone, rather than alone with these two men. "Really, no one should be talking about it at all."

Angie glanced at her watch, wished them a good afternoon, and started to walk away across the arena.

"Would you like me to walk you to your car?" Tony called after her.

A few minutes before, Angie would have thought it was nice of him to offer. Now she thought he or anyone else associated with the barn might be a murderer.

"No, thank you. I'll be alright," Angie looked back to smile at him, but really to make sure neither one of them was following her.

As she got to her car, she glanced at the arena where Reyna had died. A bright flash from the trees across the field on the other side of the ring made her jump and step backward. She stared, trying to see if there were detectives working around the creek where the shot was said to have come from, but she didn't see anyone.

Curiosity overrode her nervousness. She walked past the outdoor arena, through the pasture gate and across the field to the trees lining the creek. There was no one there. She looked up where she thought the flash had come from and saw something shiny in the branches of a tree above her.

The tree had small sturdy branches and was easy to climb. She clambered up several feet and retrieved a St. Francis medallion, hanging by its broken chain.

She went back toward her car in a daze. She couldn't find her cell phone and thought she might have left in her tack trunk. Staring absently at the pendant she carried, Angie went back into barn. She stood by the phone in the lounge wondering who she should call.

"You're not going to call anyone."

Angie almost screamed. Corey was standing halfway between the door to parking lot and the door into the barn. His serious expression was so out of character that she hardly recognized him.

He was staring at the chain in her hand. She kept her eyes on him and tried to figure out how she could get past him and out of the barn.

"Did you kill her?" Angie asked, moving toward the barn door, keeping her body turned toward him.

Corey shrugged, not looking remorseful. "She saw Grace's papers while I was registering him for the show and found out that I didn't own him. I didn't know Martin would let me keep Grace and I couldn't risk losing my horse."

As Angie neared the door and reached behind her to open it, Corey grabbed her, his free hand holding an open pocket knife.

She was familiar with the knife; he used it around the barn for everything from cutting open hay bales to fixing tractor equipment. The blade was long and had a raggedly serrated edge. She had once heard someone refer to it as a "fish-gutter".

As she tried to pull out of Corey's grip, someone grabbed Angie from behind and she screamed. Tony yanked her arm free of Corey's hand and threw her behind him into the barn. She landed roughly, sprawled across the floor and saw blood splatter across the open lounge door.

* * *

"What happened yesterday?" Carol asked Angie.

"We got back from our ride after it was all over and no one would tell us anything," Kim complained.

Angie was sitting on a hay bale that had been left in the barn aisle. She discovered when she woke that morning that her nerves were still frayed and promptly went to see her horse. Even though the barn was where the traumatic event had occurred, it was still the most soothing place for her.

"Were you hurt?" Carol asked. "Whose blood was all over the lounge?"

"I thought Tony had been stabbed," Angie said. "But when Corey attacked with the knife, he only managed to cut himself. Nicked an artery and blood sprayed everywhere."

"If you knew Corey had killed Reyna, why did you put yourself in such a dangerous situation?"

"I didn't know he was there," Angie said.

"His car was parked right next to yours!"

"I didn't see it. When I found the medallion, I remembered the gun and I just wanted to get to a phone."

"What gun?"

"One of the things Corey's uncle Troy gave him, a .22 rifle."

"I know you really liked him," Carol said, patting Angie's shoulder.

"We all liked him," Kim pointed out. Trying to distract her friend, she asked Angie, "Are you going riding with us today?"

"No. I'm still a little too shaky to ride. I was supposed to go with Corey and Reyna to the show grounds today to see Reyna and Grace practice. I'm going with Tony to watch him work with Terza instead."

Kim and Carol exchanged a look Angie chose to ignore as she waved and left the barn.

# Farrier's Tale

"I'm going to tell you a story," Davis said. "It's a true story, and it happened right here where we're sitting, not that long ago."

We were sitting on the porch of the century-old store, eating lunch. Davis had just finished shoeing some horses at my farm a few miles away.

"I had been shoeing some horses at a place not far from here," he said. "It was really hot and the horses were acting up and I was tired and irritable. When I finished I was thinking that I couldn't shoe worth a damn and I was gonna give it up; just quit. I was that fed up with myself and the whole business."

Davis was an excellent farrier; a perfectionist. I knew this firsthand from holding horses for him, sometimes impatiently, while he worked with a horse's foot and wouldn't be satisfied until he had it exactly as he wanted it; as good as he could possibly make it.

Davis ate some of his sandwich and stared off down the road.

"When I got through and I was coming back this way," he continued. "I decided to stop in and have Charlie fix me a sandwich. I pulled in, and there was nobody around except this old man sitting on the porch here.

"He was dressed old-fashioned and neat in clean blue overalls and a straw hat. He had a pocket watch on a chain and looked real respectable.

"I got out of my truck—of course, seeing me and my truck, anyone can tell what I do for a living—and this man says, 'You're a horseshoer.' Like I mentioned, my mood was pretty sour, so I said, 'I've been called worse.'

"The man said, 'I've shod many a horse right over there', and he pointed kinda that direction." Davis waved his hand at the road in front of us. "And he said, 'Horse shoeing is a gift. It takes knowledge and skill and patience. It's an art and you ought to be proud of who you are and what you do.' He sounded like I'd offended him.

"I said, 'Well, you're right. That's true and I need to remember that. Thank you.'
The old man smiled and nodded.

"I went in and Charlie wasn't in that day so I asked old Mr. Huff to make me a sandwich. I thought I'd come back out and talk to that old man some, 'cause I figured he must have some good stories to tell."

"I came back out and he wasn't here. I wasn't in the store but a minute, and there hadn't been any cars here except my truck. I figured he must have walked here from somewhere, so I went all the way around the building looking up and down the roads, but I didn't see him anywhere.

"I went back inside and asked Mr. Huff, 'Who was that old man I was just talking to out here?' Mr. Huff said, 'I didn't hear anybody but you. I wasn't paying much attention. I didn't know anybody else was out there.'"

Davis stopped talking and finished his lunch.

"So who was it?" I asked.

"I've talked to some people," Davis said. "And I didn't know this, but that barn right across the road used to be a blacksmith shop. When I told my friend Hardy about this, he told me that Mr. Huff's grandfather had been a blacksmith back then."

"You think you were talking to Mr. Huff's grandfather?"

Mr. Huff was not young, and I knew his father and certainly his grandfather must have died many years before.

Davis shook his head. "I don't know. I guess I never will. I do know that I've never forgotten what that man said to me, and whenever I'm having a rotten day I think about it and feel good about myself and what I do."

# Ghostie

I usually got to work before Teri; she had a much longer drive than I did. I clipped and bathed a poodle before she arrived. By the time I carried the poodle from the bathtub in the kennel room back to the grooming salon, Teri was there, clipping a schnauzer.

"Are all the dogs in that are coming in?" I asked over the noise of the clippers.

"I think so. We have a short day; just the two Hensley's Scotties, the Yorki, a Doberman that's just getting a bath and these two." Teri pointed to the poodle and the schnauzer.

I set the poodle on a table, turned the dryer on it, and went to check the appointment book. I counted the dogs and checked them off.

"Who's the Westie?" I asked.

Teri looked up from her clipping. "What Westie?"

"The one in the cage above the Doberman."

We had eight small cages in the grooming room and two large ones in the hallway. Teri turned off the clippers and I followed her out the hall. We looked at the West Highland White Terrier in the top cage. Neither of us recognized it, and we would have.

People who don't know dogs think every dog of certain breeds look exactly alike. But when you work with them, they are individuals. This one had an ear that was slightly smaller than the other and crooked but only a dog professional would have noticed.

"Is it in the book?" Teri asked.

"No."

Sometimes Alison, girl who worked at the front desk, took appointments for us. If we didn't have a lot scheduled, Alison would add them without having to notify Teri. Teri also sometimes got calls for appointments on her cell or at her house that she forgot to write in the book.

"I don't remember any calls for it," she said. "Check up front."

Teri's grooming shop was one room rented in the back of a small vet clinic that had once been a house. I went down the hall, through the exam room and out into the reception area.

Dr. Steve and Casey, the vet tech, were out on a farm call. The clinic was empty, so Alison was reading magazines and holding a puppy that was in for boarding.

"Is the Westie in the hall cage a patient?" I asked.

"I don't think so," Allison said. "Casey or Steve might have brought it in, but they wouldn't need one of your cages. We have plenty of room."

Alison called Casey's cell phone, and was told Casey and Steve hadn't seen the dog.

She checked their appointments, but there was nothing about a Westie.

"Is it a regular?" Alison asked. "Do you recognize it?"

"No, and if it's a new addition for one of the owners we groom for, we don't know about it."

I returned to Teri and shared what Alison said. We looked at the dog again. His coat was in good shape; it clearly got brushed regularly.

"Should we groom it?" I asked

Teri pulled the dog out of the cage and he rested comfortably in her arms.

"He doesn't need trimming and his nails look good. Let's bathe him and brush him out. I don't want to do any clipping without instructions," Teri said.

I removed the few small tangles from his fur before taking him to the tub for a bath. He was quiet and cooperative, didn't mind having the dryer blowing on him, held still for me to brush his coat out.

Teri and I were finished by noon. We cleaned up and got ready to leave. Most of the dogs we groomed got picked up later in the afternoon, so Alison brought the dogs up for the owners and collected payments.

On my way out I noticed the Westie was gone. I went to the front desk where Teri had stopped to buy some flea spray.

"Someone picked up the Westie," I said. "Who's was it?"

"Is it gone?" Teri asked.

"It didn't pass through here," Alison said.

There was only one back door to the clinic and it was kept locked. Alison went to the exam room to ask Steve or Casey if they saw the dog leave.

"No. This place is so small, it would be hard for an animal to come or go without someone seeing it."

The six of us searched the entire building and didn't find the dog.

"Well, unless someone turns up looking for it, I guess we don't need to worry about it," Dr. Steve said.

We all worried anyway.

\* \* \* \*

Teri arrived at work before me the next morning. I stopped up front and listened to Steve telling Alison about the emergency horse call he'd gone to the previous evening.

"Did anyone come in yesterday afternoon, looking for the Westie?" I asked.

"Nope," Alison said. "And I asked all the grooming clients when they came in to pick up their dogs if they had brought it in for grooming. Maybe I shouldn't have. Some of them looked concerned that we had an animal unaccounted for. I'd hate for our clients to think we're irresponsible."

Teri came in from the grooming room, holding a handful of checks and money.

"We have checks for all the dogs yesterday and fifty dollars in cash," she said. "Who did the cash come from?"

"I didn't take any cash," Alison said.

"Maybe it was for the Westie," Casey suggested.

"No one picked up the Westie."

"And no one left the money," Casey said. "The money appeared, the dog disappeared. It works out."

\* \* \* \*

Three weeks later, the dog we nicknamed Ghostie showed up again in the same cage. No one saw him come in or go out and again there was cash with the checks in the desk drawer that no one claimed to have put there.

Every three weeks he came in, and every time we thought we would figure it out and didn't.

"Know anyone who wants a kitten?" Alison asked as I walked in the door one Friday.

"Another orphan?"

"Yeah. It was hit by a car, but isn't badly hurt. It should be fine in a day or two."

I went back to the cages in the exam room and found the kitten. It was a brown and tan Siamese-type with blue eyes. I put my finger through the cage bars and scratched its head. Teri came back to look at it.

"Gorgeous," she said. "Which one of us will end up with it if we don't find it a home?"

"None of us needs any more animals," I said.

That was true. When a cat or dog came in that we couldn't adopt out, one of us always took it home.

A week later I put the kitten in my car to take home with me, just until I could find it a permanent home.

My usual route home was blocked by road construction. The detour was a complicated path over unfamiliar back roads, some of them gravel and dirt. I wasn't surprised when one of my tires went flat.

I pulled over in front of a small, white house and changed the tire. The kitten watched me through the car window, attracting a small girl from the house.

"Cute kitten," she said.

"Yes. Know anyone who might want it?" I asked.

"Lady down the street might. Her name is Annalee."

"Do you know which house?"

"Gray house at the end of the street. Big house, big yard, white fence, lots of trees."

"Does she have cats or dogs?"

"Lots."

I drove slowly up the road and found the gray house. It was ancient, but neatly kept, surrounded by a sturdy picket fence. It had a huge porch adorned with three dogs, all well-cared for and healthy.

I carried the kitten up to the porch. The dogs were friendly and polite. They weren't upset by the kitten and she wasn't excited by being surrounded by strange dogs.

My light knock on the door was answered by a small woman who looked as old as the house. She had masses of wrinkles, but didn't look frail. I introduced myself and she invited me in. Several beautiful cats of every variety were lounging in the front room.

"I work at a vet clinic and we're looking for a home for this abandoned kitten," I said. "One of your neighbors said you might want her. She's been spayed and wormed and had all her first shots."

"She's lovely," Annalee said.

She reached for the kitten and I gently handed it to her. She held it for a few minutes, the kitten purring louder by the second.

"I believe I can keep another cat," she said.

She set the kitten on the floor among the other cats scattered at our feet. They sniffed at the kitten and accepted her without fuss. That was unusual, but not astonishing.

I had no doubt the kitten would be happy and cared for.

Annalee walked to my car with me, telling me about her dogs and cats. I looked back at the collection of pets on the porch and saw a familiar dog sitting among them. I would have recognized Ghostie even without the unmatched ears.

"Hey," I said, "That's the dog we—"

I stopped and looked around. The little woman had disappeared.

# Healing

Steven sat on the back steps of the restored farm house, staring at the empty barn behind it. He looked around the pasture that formed an L-shape on the back and north side of the property. It sloped gently downhill from the yard to the creek that marked the property line. It was just what he and Sara had wanted.

His parents were inside the house shuffling boxes around. He sensed them occasionally looking out at him through the back windows. They had moved here trying to help him heal. He wanted desperately to help them recover, too, but he couldn't.

"It would help us for you to be alright," his mother said. "If you could just do *something*."

His parents had never missed a competition, his or Sara's, since he and Sara had gotten their horse, Cheyenne. While they competed with the same horse, they participated in vastly different sports. Steven rode in barrel racing and Sara did Eventing.

He and his twin had always helped each other prepare, watched each other compete and cheered each other on. They had arguments about losing each other's stuff and how to mesh their show schedules and making sure Cheyenne got enough rest and exercise between competitions.

Out in the pasture, there was a big, solid log lying beside the creek. Steven and his parents and the dog, Jiminy had watched Sara and Cheyenne approaching an obstacle that looked just like that log with a ditch in front of it. It had been a perfect day for an event, clear and cool, with no slippery grass or mud to contend with.

Somehow, Sara and Cheyenne got to the jump all wrong. Cheyenne barely cleared the ditch, crashed into the log and flipped over. Steven felt rather than saw Sara's neck break. It was like lightening, ripping him in half.

He had pulled his shattered fragments together and run to Sara, aware of how still she was, of his parents beside him, of Cheyenne thrashing weakly on the ground with one of her legs obviously broken....

"Maybe if you got another horse..." his dad said.

Steven refused. His school grades went from honors to nearly failing. His parents didn't say a word. They moved to this old house, far from their friends. Steven hardly noticed.

He wanted to help his parents; they were hurting at least as much as he was. He'd heard somewhere that a way to survive grief was to work on letting others do things to comfort you and act like it made a difference. He couldn't even do that for them.

The barn was unpainted, weathered gray-brown, with a rusting tin roof. It had two stalls and a room for tack, feed and storage. One side held a tractor and other large, unfamiliar pieces of farm equipment. Package deal, the sales agent had said; everything on the property comes with the house.

His parents came out onto the back porch. They had been watching him staring at the barn, with what they hoped was some kind of interest, instead of despair. Looking at it, Steven didn't actually feel anything.

"Maybe we could check it out a little better," his dad suggested.

Steven got up and walked across the yard with them, holding his mom's hand.

"Seems solid enough," his mom said, looking dubiously at the walls and roof.

"It is," Dad said. "And the equipment doesn't look like much, but it all works. Guess we have to learn to use this stuff."

Steven hadn't been in the barn before. He sensed something about it that caught his attention, but he couldn't pinpoint what it was. It was something that seemed wrong to him, like a sound or smell....

His parents noticed his awareness and watched him for a moment. Steven looked down at Jiminy. The dog didn't react to anything in the barn, so Steven shook off the feeling and they all retreated quietly to the house.

His parents went back to unpacking and Steven and the dog sat back on the porch steps. He stared at the barn and decided it was a smell he had recognized, but still couldn't place it.

The sun glinting off a bright object distracted him. Beside him, Jiminy whined. A chestnut horse appeared from behind the barn. It was not a dark, reddish-brown chestnut, but a lighter red-gold; coppery, the same color Cheyenne had been. Sorrel.

He heard Sara's voice in his head. "Only western horses are sorrel. In English riding, all red horses are chestnut, whatever the shade."

Looking closely, Steven could tell the horse was a mare. She had one white sock and three full stockings on her legs, where the white went all the way to her knees. She had a thin, nearly rectangular stripe of white down her face.

Her coat was shaggy and unkempt, but the parts where the winter hair had shed out were glossy. Her mane hung in ragged tangles down past her shoulder. Her tail and forelock had brambles caught in them. Her hooves were long and cracked and she was hugely overweight.

She walked slowly and smoothly up to the narrow wooden gate between the yard and the pasture. Her eyes were bright and her ears pricked forward.

She nickered. Steven didn't move.

The mare shook her head and whinnied. When Steven remained still she nuzzled what passed for a gate latch—a chain hooked to a smooth nail—and the gate swung open.

Steven heard his parents come out of the house and stand on the porch behind him. The mare came into the yard, moving gracefully—incongruous to her appearance and her split hooves—and crossed the grass to the porch.

Steven stood up and backed away. The porch was narrow and he bumped into his parents. The mare stopped at the porch, which had no railing, and stretched her neck to toward Steven, easily reaching his chest.

Steven reached out to push her away, but instead he hesitantly stroked the mare's soft, whisker-ridden muzzle.

His parents were as stunned as he was.

"The agent should have mentioned…," Dad said.

Steven stepped off the porch and pulled up some of the tall grass. He glanced at the mare's teeth as she lipped it off his palm.

"That looks like a large vet expense on legs," mom said, not sounding upset at all.

"She's not really," Steven said. "She looks rough but some grooming and regular hoof care will fix that. She's unfit, but her coat and her eyes are bright. And she's young, only about seven."

She was short, her back barely higher than Steven's shoulder. He patted her neck and ran his hand along her back. She was compact, with strong, straight legs.

"Comes with the house," Steven thought.

She had the perfect build for a barrel racer.

# Lame Excuse

I watched Ritzy trot, lame on her right front, and wasn't the least surprised. If Guy was surprised, he didn't show it. He was very professional, doing his job, rarely questioning anything or commenting unless asked.

"Should I call the vet?" he asked, when I told him to bring Ritzy to a walk.

I shook my head. I pressed Ritzy's shoulder with my fingers and she jerked away.
I knew Dr. Trent would say she had a deeply bruised muscle.

"Put her in a paddock by herself for a few days. Give her a gram of bute twice a day," I said.

It was exactly what the vet would have said to me; had in fact told me to do for a similar lameness in Forte the month before.

Bute was the common anti-inflammatory and pain reliever I thought of as 'horse aspirin'. Guy knew how to treat sore muscles as well as I did, but he would never presume to do anything without checking with me.

Guy took Ritzy into the barn and carefully wrote the instructions on the marker board for Lorry and Vern, who shared part-time shifts with him. Guy specifically wrote that the instructions were dictated by me—as if he thought Lorry or Vern wouldn't follow them if they thought I hadn't said to.

He was comfortable relying on his co-workers here, but he had come to me from a less than ideal working environment. His last employer, Don Selma, was a skunk and I suspected many of the people Guy worked with at Don's place were untrustworthy.

The horse trailer was already hooked up to the truck and loaded with Asia's show things. As soon as Guy finished the morning barn chores and left for the day, I got Asia from her stall and she loaded quietly into the trailer.

I left a note on the board saying that due to Ritzy's sudden lameness, I took Asia to the show at Deerfield. I wondered how Lorry, Guy, Vern and Alice would react to that. Whoever was responsible had lamed the wrong horse.

I had decided to take Asia to the Deerfield show three weeks previously, when Forte had gone lame two days before she was scheduled to compete.

"Strained muscle," Dr. Trent had said. Not suspicious unless you linked it with Value's illness the day before her planned show date and Salute's bruised hoof three days before his.

I had openly stated I was taking Ritzy to a show in Parsons this weekend, while secretly planning to show Asia at Deerfield; and Ritzy had come up lame.

Asia placed second in each of her three classes, all of which had a large number of entries. I was pleased that the only horse to beat her was a stunningly talented gray mare.

When I returned home, I was surprised to find Lorry had waited at the barn for me to come back from the show to help unload and unpack.

"It's too bad about Ritzy getting hurt," Lorry said. "How did Asia do?"

"Wonderful. She place second showing against John Curd's and Abby Lott's horses."

Lorry's brief smile was a nice change from her habitual scowl. She was perpetually grouchy toward people, saving her kindness and patience for the horses. If she wasn't able to work with horses and have a few of her own, I didn't know how she would survive.

Lorry's horses were nice, but she continually showed them at higher levels than they were ready for and was frequently disappointed. She also insisted on having two good-but-not-great horses, instead of investing in just one exceptional horse.

She petted and fussed over Asia proudly as she settled the mare into her stall. I wondered if it was a comfort or an irritant to Lorry that my horses continually performed well and won. Would that be a motive for her to sabotage their showing possibilities? I just couldn't imagine her hurting a horse for any reason.

"It was a big show," I said. "I was surprised Alice wasn't there."

"She took her gelding to the show in Parsons. He placed low, but that's better than he has been doing. Alice was probably surprised not to see you there."

Lorry worked for Alice a few hours a day, as well as for me and taking care of her own horses that she kept at a friend's farm.

Alice had several horses that often competed at the same shows and in the same classes as mine. Except on the surface, we didn't like each other much. She was the most likely person to want to hurt my horses' chances to show. She could walk from her farm to mine and often came over to visit, as if we were friends. She also had plenty of opportunity to harm my horses between the varying shifts of my three part-time employees, while I was chaperoning at Girl Scouts or helping at a Pony Club Rally.

The following day I was glad to see Deb, another neighbor and a true friend, at the high school where we were supervising the scenery painting for an upcoming play. Deb's daughter, Tammy, like the kids of the other chaperones, was part of the drama club.

I was anxious for children of my own, but not having found a man who was more interested in me than my money, that hadn't happened yet. The result was my large collection of horses and spending all my free time volunteering at functions with other people's kids.

The drama students knew what they were doing and Deb, I and the other parents and teachers were really only there for emergencies and occasional consultation. Deb and I got some coffee and perched on an extra table to watch the activity.

"How's Tammy's new pony?" I asked her.

"Fabulous! They are such a great team. Cabernet is a really nice change from Raffles. She was such a bad-tempered little thing."

"Geldings are generally thought to be nicer than mares," I pointed out.

"I heard about Ritzy's lameness," Deb said. "How many times is this now?"

I sighed. "Too many."

"Is it always the same thing?"

"Not always, but the same thing has happened a few times. I had Salute entered in a show last month and he went lame three days before. Dr. Trent diagnosed a bruised hoof, which could be caused by anything."

Deb nodded.

"Two days before Value's show, she came out of her stall very lethargic. She didn't have a temperature and her appetite was okay, but she seemed exhausted. She wasn't better the next day, so she didn't show.

"I didn't get suspicious until Forte was troubled by sore—maybe strained but possibly bruised—muscles the day before her competition. That's similar to the problem with Ritzy yesterday."

"It certainly sounds like someone's doing something," Deb said. "Could it be one of your help?"

"It could be, but my prime suspect is Alice. We're not close, but we compete together a lot."

"And she loses," Deb said.

Alice was Deb's neighbor, too. I didn't know how close she and Alice were, so I tried to never show how much I disliked our mutual acquaintance.

Someone called out, "We need more paint and glitter."

"Ann's bringing it. She's on her way here," I called back

Deb said, "So you took Asia this weekend."

"Yes. I didn't tell anyone. I packed Asia's things, but made sure everyone thought I was planning to show Ritzy."

"Lorry sometimes competes against your horses and loses too," Deb said. "What about the other two? I don't really know them."

"Vern and Guy have nothing to gain by hurting my horses. Guy used to work for Don Selma, who is completely unscrupulous. Guy cares for the horses so well; I don't know how he tolerated Don."

"People work where they can," Deb said, although she had no more experience with a working person's life than I did. "Don fired Guy, didn't he? Did Guy finally confront Don about the way Don handled the horses?"

"Actually, it was me and a few other people who raised a fuss about how Don's horses were always nervous and that we suspected abuse. Don pinned the blame on Guy and fired him. I thought that was unfair and would make it hard for Guy to get another job. Lorry and Vern needed some help, so I took him on. I can't imagine he had anything to do with mistreating Don's horses."

"Don is a weasel," Deb agreed. "What about Vern?"

"Vern is sweet and loves the horses. I trust him as much or more than I trust anyone. I only worry about him because he's kind of …"

Deb nodded, keeping me from having to find a polite phrase for Vern's lack of intellect.

"He occasionally helps Alice with her horses when Lorry is busy showing her own. He's so careful about following directions explicitly that I'm afraid if someone told him to do something not to tell anyone, he would to it."

"Someone like Alice," Deb said. "They must have noticed a pattern. Have any of them said anything?"

"No, but that doesn't really surprise me. Guy makes a point to just do his job and not get involved, maybe because of what happened at Don's. Lorry's so wrapped up in her own issues that if she's aware of anyone else's problems, she's likely to just be glad they're sharing what she sees as her bad luck. I don't think poor Vern has noticed anything."

The party was breaking up. The scenery looked good and it was getting late.

"What will you do?" Deb asked.

"I don't know. Keep everyone guessing about which horse is showing next and hope they don't get frustrated and hurt the horses badly or all at once."

"Or hurt you," Deb said. "That would keep your horses out of competition for awhile."

Deb's parting words were less than comforting and she was gone before I thought to ask how she had heard about Ritzy's lameness.

* * *

I was in the barn office writing paychecks when Vern came in and sat down.

"Lindsay, you were planning all along to take Asia yesterday, weren't you?" he asked.

I was seized by irrational panic. I adored Vern. I didn't want him to be in any way responsible, deliberately or otherwise.

"You knew something would happen to Ritzy," he said. "It's happened two or three times now—that you planned to take a horse somewhere and they couldn't go because of some kind of hurt or sickness. You haven't said anything about it, but is there something we can do? Me, Lorry or Guy?"

I had underestimated Vern. Because he was shy and uneducated, people, me included, thought he was slow. Maybe he was, but not stupid.

"It might be one of them that are hurting the horses," I said.

"Lorry or Guy wouldn't do that," he said.

I added naïve to my mental impression of Vern. He couldn't fathom not trusting people he liked.

"It could be Alice," I said. "Or someone I haven't thought of."

"Is there some way I can help?" he asked.

"Yes. I'm planning to take Salute to a show in Fairview next weekend. Can you try to make sure nothing happens to him?"

"Yes, I will," he said.

"Thank you." I handed him his paycheck.

When he left, I began to fill out a show entry for Salute and left it half-completed on the desk. I filled out a show entry for Value and took it with me to put in the mail.

I spent the week helping the local 4-H group with their livestock projects and worrying about my own livestock. I worked with all my horses as usual, watching them carefully for signs of unsoundness or illness.

I wasn't terribly concerned about the show points my horses weren't earning, although that seemed to be my adversary's objective. I was anxious about their welfare. My horses were valuable, but that wasn't the issue either. They had great temperaments, were affectionate as well as talented and I loved them. Whoever was doing this could easily hurt one of them seriously or permanently.

By Thursday, even though all seemed well, I was apprehensive. I was gone from the barn a lot and for once wished I didn't have so many commitments. I would have worried less if I'd know Vern was spending most of every day at the barn and all night in the hayloft above Salute's stall.

I didn't learn of this until he called my cell phone at almost midnight, just as I was returning home from a meeting.

"Lindsay, it's Vern," he nearly whispered. "I'm here at the barn—"

"Why? What happened?"

"Nothing serious," he assured me. "But you told me to keep an eye on Salute, so I wanted to check. Guy is here and he's got Salute galloping in the round pen. Is he's supposed to do that?"

"No, he's not! Does he know you're there?"

"I don't think so."

"Don't let him know. I'll be right there."

I cut off my car headlights and cruised around the house and back to the barn. I parked and got out of the car as quietly as possible.

My round pen was located behind the barn, mostly blocked from sight by the large machinery shed. As I went around the shed, I could see Guy clearly enough in the near darkness, keeping Salute moving although the horse was slowing from tiredness.

I had my cell phone in my hand and meant to call the sheriff, but anger at seeing my weary horse distracted me.

"What are you doing?" I yelled.

If Guy was startled, he didn't show it and didn't reply. He allowed Salute to stop, dropping the whip he'd been holding to encourage the horse to keep moving forward.

"What difference does it make to you whether my horses show or not?" I asked as he hopped over the fence of the round pen. "You don't have any horses to show against mine."

"Don Selma does," Guy said. "It makes a difference to him."

"What?"

"When you caused all that trouble for Don, he lost a lot of his business and he got banned from certain farms and show grounds. If he couldn't compete with his horses, he wanted to make sure your horses couldn't compete either."

"You're working for Don? He sent you over here to damage my animals?" I said.

"That's right."

I was so furious that for a moment I couldn't move or even speak. When I realized Guy wouldn't be admitting this if he thought I would be able to tell anyone, he was right in front of me.

His fist connecting with the side of my head was as bad as any impact I've suffered falling from a horse. Only terror of what he would do to me kept me from completely losing consciousness.

As I felt Guy dragging me across the ground, I learned the roaring in my ears and the flashing lights I saw weren't from concussion. They were the arrival of sheriff's deputies, summoned by Vern. Vern helped me up off the ground as the officers chased off in the direction Guy had bolted.

"I hope you heard what he said," I told Vern.

"Yes, ma'am. Voices carry out here where it's quiet." He showed me his phone. "I called the law from the barn phone. Then came out here and used my phone to record everything you and Guy said."

I hugged him. "Vern, you're a genius."

# Last Words

"The Moran family lived here in the late 1800's and around 1902 they all disappeared."

Mom was riveted by her friend's story about their newly acquired home, but I had been politely listening only because Stephanie said the Moran family was devoted to horses. I was in my senior year of college and I had a few horses of my own that I didn't get to spend enough time with.

When Stephanie mentioned the disappearance, I looked around the place with more interest.

The house was built like a castle; made of gray and tan stone with large, open rooms, dozens of windows, rounded doorways and balconies inside and out. The furniture was antique and oriental rugs covered the floors.

"After the family's disappearance," Stephanie said. "For several decades the house was empty. As time went on and people became less superstitious and it was cleaned up and sold. And then re-sold and sold again; even rented a few times, but none of the owners or renters would stay. It was empty for a long time again before it was restored and put on the market once more. We bought it six months ago and we're very comfortable here."

Stephanie's story was interrupted by footsteps running up one of the many staircases. It was hard to tell exactly where in the house the sound was, making it easy to think of ghosts. The sound came toward us and into the room where we were sitting, accompanied by a person. He looked real enough, unless the ghosts here wore jeans and t-shirts.

"My nephew, Chris," Stephanie introduced us. "This is my old college friend, Robin, and her daughter, Beth."

"Hi." Chris smiled at us quickly. He didn't find me nearly as interesting as I found him.

"Aunt Steph, were you serious when you told Win he could get a puppy for his birthday? Mark's Great Dane had a litter of puppies last month and he said I could have first pick, now that their ready."

"Great Danes?"

"Win likes big dogs," Chris said.

"We have plenty of room," Stephanie said. "I don't see why not."

"I'll go pick one out now and have it here when he gets home from school." Chris kissed his aunt and started out the door, then looked back at me. "Do you like puppies? Would you like to go with me?"

I did like puppies and wanted to go with him. I told mom and Stephanie that I would see them later and went down the stairs with Chris. It was odd, since we had never met, but I felt comfortable with Chris, as if I'd known him a long time. I was sure it had something to do with the house. The property had a strange atmosphere, as if extraordinary occurrences there would not seem unusual.

As Chris opened the car door for me I noticed how quiet it was around the house. The house, surrounded by ten acres, most of it behind the house, was now in the middle of an urban subdivision that had grown up around it. Yet there was no noise from passing cars, children playing or neighborhood dogs barking. In the absence of other sounds, the birds and wind in the huge, ancient trees seemed loud.

Pulling out of the drive was like exiting a silent hospital into a busy city street. Even with the car windows up I heard all the sounds that had been missing: kids laughing, music playing, a jet passing overhead.

Chris grinned at me. "Weird, isn't it?"

I looked back toward the house. "What's with that place?"

I expected him to tell me how the big trees around the house blocked out the sound, but the lack of noise wasn't the only unusual thing about the house.

"It's enchanted," Chris said.

"Why do you say 'enchanted', not 'haunted'?"

"Because it's peaceful."

I didn't agree. "It's quiet, but it's a heavy stillness; more like ominous."

Chris shrugged. "Could be."

"What do you do?" I asked.

I'd heard somewhere that it was rude to ask that question; that people tended to judge and stereotype others by their profession. I wondered if it was true, which was one of the reasons I always asked.

"I own a lawn care business. You?"

"Last year of college. We're on spring break this week."

"What are your favorite and least favorite classes?" he asked.

"My favorite is English. This semester my least favorite is Economics. The professor seems to think it's simple, but I just don't get it."

The drive to his friend Mark's house was short. I hardly acknowledged meeting Mark, but I got the impression he was used to having his presence eclipsed by his dogs.

The puppies were adorable and there were a lot of them. Most were black, three were fawn and one was brindle.

"I want a black one," Chris said.

All the blacks were female, but Chris said that didn't matter, which surprised me. I didn't have a dog, but when looking for horses to buy, color was the least important issue, while gender was a primary concern.

Chris chose, or was chosen by, the largest one. Her feet were enormous. She looked like a child trying to walk in her father's shoes.

Chris thanked his friend and loaded me and the puppy, who took up most of my lap, back into the car.

"We need to name her," Chris said.

"Shouldn't he get to pick the name of his dog?"

"It's not only his dog."

I gathered naming the dog was Chris's small claim to part ownership.

"Win likes exotic, foreign sounding names," Chris said. "Can you think of one?"

"Nikita."

"That fits her," he said, looking at the puppy.

With the issue of her name settled, the puppy yawned, sprawled in my lap and went to sleep. Her snoring kept us laughing all the way back to the Lawrence's house.

Nikita seemed lost when we brought her into the house. We set her down in the room where mom and Stephanie were still sitting. The puppy stood perched on her big feet, staring around the enormous room and up at the high ceiling.

I wondered if she felt anything. Animals are supposed to be sensitive to paranormal things, but Nikita showed no signs of distress.

"I'm glad we have a big house and yard," Stephanie said, surprised at the size of the puppy.

Visible through the trees in the front yard, a school bus stopped at the end of the driveway. A boy, a miniature of Chris about twelve years younger, sprinted up the driveway. He charged into the house, up the stairs, and into the room. He stopped in surprise when he saw there was company.

"This is my brother, Win," Chris said.

"I'm very pleased to meet you," Win said. He came over to us and shook hands with mom and me. Charming manners for a kid that age.

Drawn to his small size, Nikita trotted over to Win and sprawled at his feet. Win stared at the dog in confusion.

"There's a goat in the house," Win said.

"It's a puppy," Chris told him.

Win sank to the floor next to Nikita. "It *is* a puppy! Is it ours?"

"Yes." Chris settled on the floor next to his brother.

"What's his name?" Win asked.

"*Her* name is Nikita."

"That's a great name. Who picked that?"

"Beth did." Chris looked at me. "Do you know anything about training dogs?"

"Nothing, sorry. I only know about training horses."

"That's okay," Win said. "She's gonna be huge. You'll never know the difference."

We all went downstairs and into the yard to watch Win and Nikita get acquainted, romping on the enormous lawn. We met Stephanie's sons, Seth and Cord, and their respective wives, Alice and Sally, as they arrived home from various jobs. The entire family resided together. The house was so large, it only seemed practical.

They all adored Win, as there were no other young children in the family. Everyone was delighted with the puppy.

Nikita proved to be quite smart, and after I did some research on dog training I was able to help Win and Chris get started teaching her. I spent much of my week off with the Lawrences, so I was there when things got strange. It started with Stephanie.

Everyone was home, gathered in the large kitchen, where Chris was telling me about the stable at the back of the property.

Stephanie said, "We all love to ride."

I was surprised. Everyone else was stunned.

"*What?*" Cord asked.

"What did I say?" Stephanie asked.

"That we all love to ride," Seth said.

"Horses?" Stephanie frowned. "That's odd. No one in this family has ever been fond of riding, least of all me. I barely have enough coordination to play checkers."

Win snorted and giggled, making us laugh. They were a close family and they laughed a lot.

"Beth, you haven't seen the stable yet," Chris said. "Would you like to now?"

"Not today, thanks. I need to go. Spring Break or not I still need to study. Maybe next time."

Chris leaned close to me and whispered, "I'm a great economics tutor."

"That's good to know," I said, seriously. "Because I'm the world's worst economics student."

I found myself at the Lawrence's several nights a week learning economics. The first evening, when Chris and I needed a break, he, Keeta and I went out to see the stable. The barn was built of the same stone as the house and the wood interior was well preserved wood. The whole structure was thick with dust and cobwebs, but everything had been put in order before it was vacated.

There was still straw bedding in the stalls and hay in the mangers. I was only absently aware of how odd that was, possibly because it was familiar. At the fancy barn where I boarded my horses, everything was always in perfect order, waiting for the horses to be brought in from the pastures.

It should have been bizarre, but it seemed natural under the spell of the house and property. I remembered that Chris had used the word 'enchanted' to describe the house. It did seem that some kind of magic was present.

"What happened to the horses? Did they die?" I asked.

"I guess they were sold. I don't think they would have been left here. Why would you think they died?"

"This reminds me of a book," I explained. "A Mary Stuart novel, Airs Above the Ground. I don't remember what country it was, but they had a tradition that when a beloved horse died they always kept its place in the barn prepared anyway. To show respect for its memory or something."

Each stall had an engraved wooden plaque with the horse's name and the name of the family member that rode it.

"There's no stall for Adam's horse," I said.

"Who's Adam?"

"Some tour guide you are! According to Stephanie, there were seven Morans. Three brothers; Frank, Adam and Sebastian and their father, Prentice, and two sisters, Vivian and Emilene. None of the stalls have Adam's name."

Chris' face was blank as he stared at one of the nameplates.

"No," he said. His voice sounded strange. "Emilene said we all love to ride, but I never have."

He glared at me with such venom that I took a step backward and Keeta growled.

"Chris?" Alice's voice came from the barn doorway.

"Yes, ma'am?" Chris answered.

"Sally made a cheesecake. You two should come have some."

"You like cheesecake?" Chris asked. He held out his hand to me and we walked back to the house.

I hadn't played checkers in years, but a few days later I was cajoled into joining the Lawrence Family Checkers Championship of the Universe Tournament. I played the first round against Chris and lost quickly and easily. Chris smirked at my bad moves and jumped my last three checkers all in one move.

We watched the others play with good-natured competitiveness, until Cord and Sally's match.

"You take too long to decide your moves, Vivian," Cord complained.

"I don't want to play like Sebastian and lose because of carelessness," Sally replied.

"I almost never lose!" Win protested.

"You lose all the time, liar," Seth told him.

"Don't call him a liar, Frank," Stephanie said.

I glanced at Chris, who was staring at the others with the same look of hatred I'd seen on his face at the barn.

"Who's competing in the first set of playoffs?" I asked, louder than necessary. Everyone looked at me.

"We know it isn't you," Win said, cheerfully.

I was relieved to hear the group's familiar laughter.

The episode a few days later was worse. Cord, Seth, Alice and Sally were planning to take Win on a weekend camping trip. They were listing what they needed to pack, concentrating on things they were most likely to forget.

"Matches."

"Flashlight."

"Bug spray," Stephanie suggested.

"Horse feed," Sally said.

"We wouldn't forget that," Seth answered, sharply.

Alice interrupted before an argument could ensue. "Will this trip be too much for Sebastian's pony? He's getting old for this sort of thing."

"We'll go slowly," Cord said. "Frosty will be fine."

It was like being in a room with several insane people. Win was listening, but didn't seem confused or alarmed. Stephanie was unconcerned. Chris had the same frightening scowl I'd seen twice before.

"Adam, while we're gone you—"

"Don't tell me what to do," Chris snapped. "I'm not a servant! Just because I don't like horses, that doesn't mean I'm not a member of the family."

"If you were a member of this family, you would learn to ride and come with us." Cord grabbed the front of Chris's shirt.

"Don't you hit him, Prentice!" Stephanie's voice stopped everything.

Cord let go of Chris, and they all looked around at each other, as if aware for the first time that something had happened. The silence was awkward.

"I have to go," I said, quietly.

"I'll walk you to your car," Chris said.

When we were standing in the driveway I asked Chris, "Were you aware of what was going on in there?"

Chris stared at the ground for several seconds.

"Sort of. It's kind of like being in a play, I guess. You get so caught up in the plot that you act without thinking about it. I'm sorry if we scared you."

It did scare me, especially if they had no control over it.

"Will you go to the library with me tomorrow?" I asked.

"Sure. School project?"

I shook my head. "I've remembered something from another novel."

We went to the main branch of the county library and looked for information about the Moran family or the house. We checked by computer and then looked through all the local history and genealogy records, but didn't find anything more than basic facts like names and dates. We asked the staff, who had no useful suggestions.

"This was a waste of time," I said.

As we head for the door, we were approached by an old woman, the oldest person I had ever seen.

"Perhaps I can help you," she said. "My grandmother worked for the Moran family."

"We're trying to find out what happened to them," I said.

"They disappeared. No one knows what happened to any of them, except for Adam."

"Adam didn't vanish with the rest of the family?" Chris asked.

The woman looked tottery, so we helped her to a chair in an empty corner of the library.

"My grandmother told me about it," the woman said. "It was something she never forgot. The family had been planning a trip, a hunting trip I think it was. All the house help had been given a holiday, except for my grandmother, who planned to stay and look after Adam. Right after the family left, Adam told her he was going to visit with friends in the next county, so grandmother could have a holiday and she went to stay with her sister.

"When she returned two weeks later, the family was gone and everything had been sold and was being cleared out of the house. Even before everyone left, a Mr. Moran, no one knew the first name, had made arrangements with a merchant from a few towns over to sell everything."

The woman's voice was strong and she didn't seem to be getting tired from telling us her story. Chris and I were riveted.

"The merchant's name was Mr. Shoat, I believe, and he was so honest and well-respected that no one doubted his word, even if he himself seemed surprised at the situation. Thing was, there weren't any Morans around to really contest it."

"As it turned out, Adam took a train out of town several days after his family left on their trip, just the day before Mr. Shoat was to arrive to take everything from the house. Incidentally, the train crashed and Adam was killed. The other family members were never heard from again."

"What about the horses?"

"They disappeared with the family. They had taken the horses and never returned. That's all we ever knew. Adam's body is buried on the property and his is the only one there. There were no other relatives, so after awhile, people stopped wondering about it."

I couldn't think of any more questions. We thanked her and left the library. It didn't occur to me until we were in the car that we should have gotten her name.

"So what do you think?" I asked Chris.

"That Adam's family didn't like him. They faked going on a hunting trip and when Adam left town to see his friends, they sold everything and moved away."

I considered that possibility briefly and shook my head.

"What's your theory?" he asked. "Something in the other book you mentioned? What was it?"

"I don't remember who wrote it, or what it was called. A woman and her niece lived together and the aunt started dating one of the niece's college professors. When the aunt, professor, niece and the niece's boyfriend were at the house together, everyone except the aunt started acting strange.

"The previous occupants of the house had been a girl and her father. The father didn't like the girl's boyfriend and the three of them fought all the time. Finally, the father killed the boyfriend. I think maybe he killed the daughter too, but I can't remember. Anyway, he buried one or both of them under the basement floor. The aunt figured out that her niece, the girl's boyfriend and the professor were reenacting what happened.

"They found the bodies and buried them properly, but the professor had almost killed the niece's boyfriend before they realized what was going on. What's happening with your family is just like that."

"Beth, that's fiction," Chris argued. "That was a ghost story you read. You think something like that happened to the Morans?"

"I think Adam murdered his family, sold their horses and everything and left town."

"That's…harsh," he said. "And there would have been records of selling that many horses, like the furniture and stuff from the house. Someone would have remembered."

He had a point, but it didn't dissuade me.

"There are obviously unrestful spirits there and they are those of the Moran family," I said. "I don't think what happened was as peaceful as the family moving away and not telling Adam about it. These little scenes you're acting out could lead to serious violence."

Chris didn't respond. He looked worried.

"We've all seen it, Chris. Think about what might happen when you and your family repeat the last words the Morans ever said to each other. We have to find a way to stop it."

"How? Convince everyone that we have to leave our new home?"

"I thought of that but I'm afraid it wouldn't work. Now that the spirits have found a family they can work with, this could continue anywhere. Or it could start again with the next residents. Maybe just finding the bodies, like they do in stories, would put them to rest."

"They haven't been found for decades."

"Maybe nobody suspected murder. It's possible no one ever looked for them."

"Where do we start?" he asked.

"I don't know. It's likely to be somewhere near the house, but I'm not familiar with the house or the grounds. Where is Adam buried? Does the house have a cellar? An old garden or a well? We should ask your family for ideas."

"Okay," Chris said, when we arrived back at the house. "We'll tell them our theory and see what they come up with."

We never even got to discuss it.

When we got back to the house none of the Lawrences were present, but all of the Morans were there. They didn't notice that "Adam" had returned or acknowledge that I existed. I listened to their discussion and arguments as they packed supplies for the trip. That they didn't get along all that well even when Adam wasn't around. When I realized Chris had vanished from my side, I began to panic.

The family started carrying things out to the barn and I followed. My cell phone was in my car, but I was afraid to let them out of my sight to go get it.

I did not want to see what was about to happen. If I couldn't stop this, how could I explain it to the police?

I thought maybe it would stop when they found no horses in the barn. That hope was short-lived. As they were crossing the yard, Chris reappeared with a shotgun.

I stood what I hoped was a safe distance apart from the others. Keeta was beside me, whining. Adam had to have planned this. What was the plan?

"What will you do with the bodies?" I asked Chris.

He ignored me and pointed the gun at Cord. The rest of the "Morans" watched him, too shocked to move. Before he pulled the trigger, I had the answer.

"They're buried in the barn!" I yelled, desperately.

Chris lowered the gun and everyone looked at me. "What?"

"When Adam shot his family, he buried each person under the floor of their horse's stall. That's why the stalls were fixed up neatly, as if ready for the horses—to hide the bodies."

It was probably also why they looked the same, even more than a century later.

Chris walked away with the gun and returned with a shovel.

Alice, Sally, Stephanie and I went into the house to avoid seeing whatever grisly things the guys might discover. Win came in and told us about it in great detail anyway.

"Guess what else they found?" he said. "The horses were buried under the barn stalls too!"

That was a shock, but I shouldn't have been surprised. As Chris had said, if they'd been left at the house or sold, someone would have noticed and remembered it. I couldn't imagine the amount of work and effort that must have taken Adam in the two weeks after the murder before he left on the train. Perhaps he found a way to hire help or his energy was fueled by his hatred and anger.

Stephanie contacted the police. There were a lot of questions to be answered and red tape to be gone through, but the Lawrences were hopeful that the Morans would eventually all be laid to rest together.

"No one cared about what happened to them when they were murdered," Seth grumbled. "Why would they care about what happens to them now?"

"We cared about them," Win pointed out.

"We didn't have much choice," I said. "You don't hate horses, do you, Chris?"

"I don't think so. Why?"

"I like to take you to meet mine."

Chris smiled.

"Can I come?" Win asked. "I can help you train Chris."

# Pictures

Tony and the dogs came looking for me. Adam, the younger and less dignified of the two dogs—meaning hyper and harebrained—found me first.

I was lying in an uncomfortable spot at the base of a tree with rocks and roots pressing into my back. My riding helmet was still firmly fitted to my head. Hearing five pairs of feet approaching, I carefully moved into a sitting position.

I was stunned, but conscious when Adam almost pounced on me. I made myself appear alert, not wanting to scare Tony. At nine, he was much more perceptive than most kids his age. And I never knew when his amazing artist's mind was going to snap a photographic memory that would reproduce itself in one of his incredible pencil or pen and ink drawings.

I sensed my horse, Walt, standing behind me next to the tree. He was calm, and therefore presumably unhurt.

"Aiimmeee!" Tony's greeting was half-panicked and half-relieved. I could gauge his level of concern by the number of vowels he pronounced in my name, which really only has two.

"I'm okay, Tony," I said, though I hadn't checked myself for damages.

I was confused, but years of experience had taught me that if I was on the ground at the feet of a saddled horse, there was a possibility of injury. The fact that my brain and vision were both a little fuzzy suggested at least a mild concussion.

Adam had stopped short of knocking me back to my prone position and was prancing around happily. Tony, light haired and freckled and short of breath from his sprint through the woods, sank down next to me as if we had gathered for a picnic.

"How are you, really?" he asked.

"Alright, I think."

"What happened?"

Walt gave a comically well-timed snort, a one-syllable derision of his rider's inability to stay in the saddle.

"I'm not sure," I said.

I had a sudden vivid memory of Walt bucking and me sailing through the air toward the tree I was sitting next to.

"Did he throw you?" Tony asked.

Tony wasn't reading my mind as much as my expression when I realized that Walt had indeed pitched me off—violently.

I twisted around painfully and looked up at Walt, who stood placidly, the way he usually did when I fell off due to my own lack of balance and coordination. He didn't look upset or uncomfortable and there was no sign of what might have made him act so out of character.

With effort I carefully stood up and looked him over. I patted his neck and ran my hands down each of his legs. I hoped Tony wouldn't notice how shaky I was.

I pulled the reins forward over Walt's head and held them over my arm while I reached up to loosen his girth. When I touched the girth strap, Walt almost jumped out of his skin.

"Easy, Walt."

He remained tense, but let me undo the girth and I gently lifted the saddle off his back. The underside of the fluffy, sheepskin pad had three huge, spiky burrs stuck to it.

"Walt, I'm sorry!" I said. He hadn't acted twitchy when I mounted or during the first part of our ride. Unobtrusive at first, the burrs must have worked their way under the saddle pad until a shift in my weight pressed them into the sensitive skin of his back, causing him to buck.

Tony's eyes widened. "Who would put burrs under your saddle pad?" he asked.

"No one put them there," I said. "They must have gotten brushed onto it by me or one of the dogs. It was my own carelessness."

Tony looked at the dogs, whose coats were speckled with burrs, twigs and leaves.

Disgusted with myself, I pulled the burrs off the saddle pad, double checked to make sure there were no others and set the saddle back on Walt, securing the girth loosely.

As we walked back to the barn, I hoped movement would ward off some the stiffness I would soon feel.

When we got to the barn, I unbuckled both sides of the girth and threw it across the top of the saddle, then pulled the saddle and pad off Walt's back. I set them on the floor instead of on one of the conveniently placed saddle racks mounted on the wall. Adam promptly settled himself on the soft fleece of the saddle pad.

Tony rolled his eyes. "Up, Adam."

The dog moved and Tony picked up the saddle pad, pulled off a few more burrs and set it on the rack along with the saddle and girth.

"What are we going to do today?" I asked Tony.

Tony usually had something in mind for us to do together on Saturdays; picnics, movies, bowling, art exhibits—things that didn't cost too much.

"It's too nice to be indoors," Tony said. "Do you feel okay enough to go to Recreation World?"

"Sure," I said. I wasn't going to let a headache and some bruises, which were my own fault anyway, keep me from it.

Our parents died two years before, when Tony—a surprise blessing for my parents twelve years after my arrival—was six. Their life insurance allowed us to keep the farm, where we boarded horses, but farm upkeep was costly and there wasn't a lot of money left over.

"Tony, what made you come looking for me this morning?"

"I asked Emily where you were and when she said you'd gone out riding, I got one of those feelings."

Despite our difference in age, Tony and I had always been close and we could each sense, even from a distance, when something was wrong with the other.

I looked out through the window and saw Emily and Jessica riding around the arena, warming up for their lesson. Emily and Joe had arrived early and been bringing in their horses when I was getting Walt ready to ride.

"Where's Joe?" I asked.

"He's soaking his horse's leg. It was swollen this morning."

I hoped nothing was badly wrong. Joe was anxious to sell his horse and was expecting some serious buyers to look at him the next day.

After a day of go-carts and miniature golf and a non-nutritious lunch at the snack bar, I did the afternoon barn chores while Tony went in to do his homework. Emily, Joe, Jessica and Natalie were still at the barn.

Joe was still fussing over his horse's leg and Emily was again telling Jessica and Natalie about the fabulous stallion her mare, Vega, was bred to.

"Did you have a fall this morning?" Emily asked me.

Although I'd kept moving, I was starting to stiffen up, and it was noticeable.

"Yes," I said. "No damage."

"What happened?" Natalie asked.

"Something upset Walt and he bucked."

"What was it?"

I shrugged. I didn't mention the burrs. I am usually straightforward about my own mistakes, and some of them are particularly stupid, but I didn't want to admit that my carelessness had hurt my horse.

"Good that you weren't injured," Joe commented. "Especially since you were alone. You shouldn't go off riding when you're alone."

"You were here," I said. "You knew I was going out with Walt."

"Still not the safest thing to do," Emily pointed out and she was right.

Tony didn't join me to help feed; I guessed he'd gotten wrapped up in a school assignment or a picture. When I finished and went up to the house, he was cooking dinner and adding touches to a new drawing on the kitchen table. It was a portrait of me sitting at the base of a tree with Adam next to me and Walt standing beside us. As always, I was amazed at my brother's talent.

"That's a great picture, Tony," I said.

I could tell he thought so too, even though like most artists he could be very critical of his own work.

The picture could have been very unflattering—me looking dazed or even sprawled at Walt's feet. Three other pictures he had done recently came to mind. One of me crashing the tractor through the wall of the machine shed; one of Joe flying through the air when his horse refused a jump and another picture of two horses mating in a field.

While I admired these pictures for their realism and artistic merit, I tried to explain to Tony what was and wasn't appropriate subject matter. Since many of his pictures were displayed locally and sometimes nationally, he conferred with me about what pictures should or shouldn't be shown to people other than myself.

A few weeks previously we'd had some of his pictures spread out in the kitchen when Joe and Emily came in to tell me that the horses had broken two fence boards. They saw the pictures of the breeding horses, the one of me on the tractor and the one of Joe falling.

They commented positively on most of the drawings, but two of the pictures made Joe and Emily uncomfortable. I couldn't tell if Joe was angry or embarrassed about the one featuring him, but Emily was flustered by the picture of the frolicking horses.

I had learned that inspiration for Tony's pictures often came from things he remembered because they triggered some kind of strong emotion. He was frightened for me today; alarmed when Joe sailed over the jump without his horse and shocked at my crashing the tractor—or possibly my language at the time. I thought he was curious, or maybe just surprised, about the behavior of the breeding horses, and we had discussed inappropriate language, tractor safety and horse reproduction.

Sunday morning Tony staggered around trying to get ready for church while I quickly did the morning feeding and turnout. Tony was not a morning person and was barely dressed by the time I changed clothes and was ready to go.

"How is Millie?" he asked.

"She's fine."

Millie was Tony's ancient pony, deemed unridable the previous year when her vision became questionable. She now lived peacefully in a large pasture at the back of the farm with two other retired horses. I checked on them twice a day when I did the morning and evening feed.

"Go with me to see her this afternoon?" Tony requested.

"Sure."

Tony hadn't shown an interest in riding other horses, but had drawn many pictures of Millie since she'd lost her sight. As much as he loved Millie, he didn't like to go see her on his own, because it made him sad.

After church we changed clothes, ate lunch and then went down to the barn, which was crowded with early afternoon riders.

"Hi, Jess," I said, as I stole an apple from her bag of horse treats.

"Help yourself," Jess said.

Tony and I were fond of apples. No one was surprised when we raided their supplies. Tony was more picky than I was and went for an apple from Emily's bag. Emily always brought the biggest and freshest apples for her horses, Vogue, Vega and Viper, but I thought she also did so with Tony in mind. Everyone was fond of Tony.

"May I have an apple please, Emily?" Tony asked, instead of just grabbing one the way I did.

"Sure." Emily smiled at him.

Tony chose a large apple and we walked toward the riding ring where Joe was riding his horse for prospective buyers from out of state.

"He's very honest about his jumping and has a great attitude," Joe said, before demonstrating by riding his horse through a tricky combination of jumps.

Tony frowned and whispered to me, "That's not always true."

Joe's horse, Garamond, known as Gary, had a great attitude sometimes. He was just as often cantankerous and uncooperative, as a certain one of Tony's pictures had exemplified. I waited to see if Joe would clarify his description of Gary, but he said nothing to lessen how impressed his audience was.

As the young man who was interested in purchasing Gary took Joe's place in the saddle, Joe looked over at us, worried that I might say something.

"Gary is really having a good day," he said to the man on Gary's back. "He can't be quite this great all the time."

If the buyers were seriously interested, I trusted Joe to be honest with them about Gary's bad days and we walked toward the far pasture.

Tony's apple was too big for him—especially to eat while walking—and he only got one small bite before he dropped it.

"Share mine," I said. "And feed that one to Millie."

Millie was standing near the gate and nickered when Tony said her name. She daintily ate the apple while Tony talked to her and rubbed her neck.

We went back to the barn where Joe was shaking hands with his visitors as they prepared to leave. Everyone looked very positive, but the glance Joe gave me and Tony hinted that he had still been less than honest about Gary's faults.

Gary was a great horse and anyone would be lucky to have him. A rider looking for a horse of Gary's caliber would certainly be good enough to handle Gary's occasional temperamental moments, but any vice would give the potential buyer room to negotiate on the price.

Tony had gotten quiet and when I asked if he was okay, he said he wasn't feeling well. I took him to the house and put him to bed. He had a stomachache and chills, but no fever. I took some paperwork into his room and stayed with him. He rested fitfully, trying to act less uncomfortable than he was.

I left him to quickly feed the horses and skipped taking grain to the back pasture, as I did sometimes did if I was in hurry. At dinner, Tony said he was feeling better and ate some soup, but he still looked pale and ill.

I stayed in his room the entire night and he slept well; better than I did.

The next morning, he said he felt fine. He still looked peaked, but wanted to go to school. I trusted his judgment, so I waited with him until the school bus picked him up.

"Call me if you start feeling sick again," I instructed.

"I promise," he said.

I fed the horses, which I usually did before sending Tony off to school, and they were cranky about my tardiness. I carried a small bucket of grain to the far pasture and found Millie lying dead near the gate.

I cried harder and longer than I would have expected, possibly because it was so surprising. She'd been fine the day before, but she *was* old. I was glad she had died peacefully, without prolonged illness and that Tony had visited her the day before.

I called a neighbor to bring his equipment over to bury her in the pasture.

When Tony came home he looked better. I fed him cookies, hugged him and told him Millie had died. His response was similar to mine: surprise, tears and gratefulness that it hadn't been a long struggle.

Feeling clingy, he followed me to the barn where Joe, Emily and Nicole were still working with their horses.

"What's wrong, Tony?" Emily asked. "Are you sick?"

"I was sick yesterday," Tony said. "I'm feeling better today."

"Millie died last night," I told them. "I found her this morning and had her buried in the pasture."

Everyone was sympathetic. Emily and Nicole hugged Tony and it made him feel better.

The next morning my trainer, Tina, came to the barn to give me a lesson. I was preoccupied and not sure why. Tony had looked much better when I sent him off to school. I decided I was still upset about Millie. I refused to think I might still be mildly concussed from my fall off Walt two days before.

I almost forgot to brush Walt's left side, but did remember to check him and my saddle pad for burrs. I got the wrong bridle and struggled with it for a few minutes before I figured out that it wasn't Walt's. Then my girth came apart as I was tightening it.

"Sorry, I'm so slow this morning," I said to Tina. "One of the buckles on the girth came loose from the leather and I had to find another girth."

"That wasn't your new girth that broke, was it?" she asked.

"Yes. I'll take it back to Gail at the tack shop this afternoon and have it repaired or replaced."

My lesson went fairly well. I was still not entirely focused, but Walt was being an angel. I suspected Tina was being easy on us and overly positive about our performance, but I appreciated it.

After lunch, I took my new—and newly broken—girth into Gail's shop. Gail studied the girth and looked at me.

"These stitches didn't come undone or break," she said. "They were cut."

She showed me the nicks in the leather where something sharp had sliced the stitches.

"That could have snagged on something," I said.

She showed me the other end of the girth, where the same nicks showed and the stitches holding the buckles were sliced. She yanked on the buckle and it came away from the leather. Something couldn't have accidentally cut the stitches on both ends of the girth.

"That's too dangerous to be a practical joke," Gail remarked.

I left the girth to be repaired, thanked Gail, and went back to my truck.

As I considered my sabotaged girth, I recalled being thrown from my horse and my brother asking, "Who would put burrs under your saddle?"

Tony had taken one bite of an apple and fed the rest of it to Millie. Hours later Tony was very sick and Millie was dead.

Someone was trying to hurt one or both of us, but why?

They hadn't necessarily meant to kill me or Tony. A serious accident or illness would have successfully distracted either of us from meddling in anyone else's business. Whose?

I thought about Joe, wanting desperately to sell his horse and concerned that Tony or I might tell someone his horse wasn't always great. Tony had a picture to illustrate it.

The apple had come from Emily's bag. Could she be involved because she and Joe were friends? Or was there another issue I wasn't aware of?

Emily and Joe had consoled Tony on the loss of his pony. What kind of people would try to poison a person and then feel bad that they poisoned a pony instead?

I didn't notice the way the old truck sputtered until it stalled altogether. Feeling completely paranoid, I wondered what had been done to it as I called the local garage. A wrecker arrived quickly and dropped me off at the house before towing the truck to the shop.

I went into the house to look for Tony, but he wasn't there. I glanced at his portfolio of drawings and had a disturbing thought.

I flipped through to the picture of the mating horses and figured it out. The horses in the picture were Emily's mare Vega and her young colt, Viper. If this picture was drawn from an actual scene, and I was certain it had been, it was proof of something Emily knew or suspected: that Vega wasn't pregnant by the expensive stallion Emily had bred the mare to, but was instead expecting a foal sired by lovable but mediocre Viper.

If Emily thought Tony or I recognized the horses in the picture and what the scene might indicate, she had good reason to want to distract me from it.

And where was Tony now? I ran into the barn and called Tony's name.

Jill stuck her head out of her horse's stall. "He isn't here. He asked me to tell you that Emily took him to get some ice cream. They just left."

I looked out and saw Emily's car turn out of the drive onto the road. Jill was always dropped off by a parent or older brother and had no car I could borrow. I couldn't chase them down the road on foot. I discarded the thought of calling the police. How long would they take? How could I explain? What would happen to Tony in the meantime?

I opened the gate of the empty front paddock, and ran to the machine shed. I leaped onto the tractor and backed it out of the shed at an unsafe speed. I maneuvered through the gate into the field, put the tractor in its highest gear and pushed the throttle forward as far as it would go.

I hadn't ever driven across a field at high speed. Riding the tractor fast over what looked like a smooth, level pasture was like sitting on a bucking rodeo horse.

Emily was driving sedately beside the front pasture that I was racing across. The road turned and followed the corner of the pasture and ran along the far side for several dozen yards before turning away from the farm.

Tony didn't see me, but Emily did. She tried to speed up, but couldn't go too fast around the ninety degree turn.

As Emily rounded the corner of the farm and I approached the fence, I turned the tractor at an angle and made use of a fact I had emphasized to Tony many times; that a tractor would keep running at whatever speed it was going, even if the driver fell off.

Hoping the tractor would continue on a straight path, I jumped off.

I don't know how fast a tractor can go at its top speed. My plan, not the least crazy part of my desperate idea, had been to jump off while it was rolling and land running along beside it, hopefully not falling under the wheels. When my feet hit the ground I realized that wasn't even a possibility. I used my vast experience with falling off fast moving horses to avoid injury.

As with falls off horses, I was surprised at the force of the impact. I tumbled several yards before regaining my feet. I staggered in a small circle before sprinting after the sound of the tractor, which was a vague shape in my blurry vision.

My sight cleared enough for me to see that my insane scheme might actually work, if only because Emily saw the driverless tractor and slowed down in either curiosity or confusion, probably not concern. She was distracted enough not to see what was about to happen.

The tractor hit the fence and plowed right through it, down the small slope to the road and directly into the path of the car. Emily hit the brakes, and tried to swerve around the front of the tractor. Since it was still moving forward without slowing, she crashed right into it.

Tony disentangled from seatbelt and airbag, scrambled out of the car and ran toward me. I reached the broken fence about the same time he did. If he hadn't grabbed me, I would have collapsed.

Tony looked around in shock at me, the broken fence, the tractor and the car.

I was gratified to see that at first glance it looked like the car took more damage than the tractor. Both vehicles had stopped on impact and I hoped the tractor wasn't beyond repair.

"It's insured," Tony said, looking at me.

I was slightly ashamed that he knew I was thinking of the tractor and not the person in the car.

She wasn't moving, but I really wasn't worried about Emily.

"She was acting really strange," Tony said. "She said she was going to find a way to make sure we never told anyone. Told what?"

Whatever I had imagined Emily meant to do, she wasn't going to tell me or anyone and I had no proof of my suspicions. I couldn't guess how this would play out, but I'd have to worry about it later. My part in it could be seen as misadventure.

"I don't know," I answered. "If anyone asks, this was just a bizarre accident."

Tony nodded without question and we headed down to the car to check on Emily.

# The Pony Doctor

"Oliver, let's go for a drink after work."

Fred made this suggestion every afternoon. Good guy that he was, Fred was intrigued that after spending the week working horrible hours at a horrible job, I didn't spend a little of my paycheck on myself.

"You need to enjoy yourself some," he said.

"I enjoy my time with my sister," I said. "Why don't you come with us this weekend? Meet us at the station tomorrow morning."

My young sister, Deborah, had become ill weeks before. With all the money I and my parents could come up with, I had taken her to see a doctor. I told my parents only that he had recommended weekly treatments, but gave no guarantee of success.

Deborah was shy with strangers, but considered any friend of mine a friend of hers. For the entire train ride, she chatted comfortably with Fred about his job at the factory where he and I worked.

The train took us out of the city, and it was a long walk from the station where we disembarked to our destination. The weather was fine and we walked slowly so Deborah wouldn't grow tired.

Mr. Gentry was a kind man who had a small farm and few ponies, which were beautiful to see after the dim grittiness of the city. For the small amount of money I could give him, he set Deborah gently on the pony of her choice. She loved all of them and chose a different mount each visit. Mr. Gentry led Deborah and the pony around the sunny green pasture while Fred and I sat under a tree and watched her smile and pet the pony's soft coat.

When Deborah began to tire, we thanked Mr. Gentry and began our walk back toward the train, Fred taking turns with me to carry Deborah part of the way.

"You make this journey every week, just for her to be led around on a pony?" Fred asked.

I shook my head. "Tell Fred what you did today, Deb."

"I rescued a princess," Deborah said. "She was kidnapped and hidden in the jungle. My pony and I had to search for her. We had to go around a swamp of alligators to get to her. Then we ran from tigers to escape and return her to the prince she was going to marry."

Fred smiled. "That's quite an adventure. What did you do last week?"

On the train ride home Deborah told us about the times she'd been a princess being escorted through the desert to meet her own prince, a pony express rider in the wilds of the frontier, a spy crossing Europe on horseback carrying important papers, a warrior and her steed doing battle against a dragon.

I don't know if my parents guessed that I knew Deborah would not get well, or even that I didn't take her to a doctor on the weekends. They did know that every Saturday she returned with bright eyes and a smile that lasted all week. When she died a few months later, I hope that her heart was lighter than it might have been. I know mine was.

Not long after we lost my sister, Fred tried again to entice me to get together with him outside of work. Dispirited as I was, I thought it couldn't hurt.

"Deborah would want you to," he said.

"What did you have in mind?" I asked.

Fred hesitated. "Our boss's boss—you know the one nobody likes?—I've heard that his son is sick and doesn't seem to be getting better. I thought maybe, if his parents agree and you and I could take him, a visit to the pony doctor might do some good."

# Somebody's Grandmother

I felt bad about bringing my bridle to Jane for her to clean, partly because it meant spending money I could have used for other things and partly because I was acknowledging the pain in my wrists.

"Hello, Sylvie," Jane said. "You usually do you own tack."

"My hands are giving me trouble," I admitted.

Jane took my bridle and hung it on one of the several, many-pronged hooks hanging by her chair. She had her own little complex system and she needed one. She cleaned dozens of bridles and saddles and other random pieces of leather every day. I made good money typing papers at the university—it was amazing to me how many people still couldn't type proficiently—but Jane probably made more money than I did.

"You're in college," she said.

"Yes. I started late. I'm twenty-five."

"Type a lot of papers?"

I nodded. "I have a full scholarship, but typing papers for other students and some of the faculty is how I earn money for my horse."

"Time to do something else, before it gets worse."

"I guess so."

Jane was good for advice or just talking to about anything. No matter what the subject, she left you feeling better about it. I couldn't guess what her age was, but certainly old enough to have gained a lot of experience and learned from it. In spite of her years, her fingers were agile and her mind was sharp. More importantly, she was kind and thoughtful.

I dreaded finding any other kind of work. I liked having something I could schedule on my own time and be paid well for it.

"When do you need your bridle done?" she asked.

"Not until Sunday afternoon or Monday. I don't think I'll get out here again before then."

Just thinking of the three papers I had to type made my hands hurt.

I watched Jane carefully look and feel over the leather of the bridle she had just finished, looking for damage or weakness, as well as making sure it was perfectly clean and supple. Some of the bridles—as well as some martingales, girths, extra reins and various other pieces of equipment she cleaned—were marked with brightly colored tags she'd written notes on about loose stitches or worn leather.

Kyle came over carrying two bridles and I smiled at him. It was impossible not to like Kyle. He was charming; kind and polite to everyone, which was something many people in the equestrian world were not.

"Hi, Sylvie. Hello, Ms. Jones. These are mine and Eduardo's."

He handed the bridles to her one at a time so she knew which was whose. Like everyone except me, Kyle thought Jane was apt to mix up the similar masses of leather she worked with. I figured she knew every piece of tack by sight and could name the owner of every bridle *and* the horse that wore it.

Kyle's uncle, Devon, owned the farm and handled all of the business decisions, but Kyle handled much of the daily management of the farm. Kyle was easygoing and friendly, particularly good at interacting with the barn patrons. Devon was also very nice, but he was six-foot six and always dressed in dark clothes, whether suits or casual clothing or even riding attire. Where Kyle was approachable, Devon was intimidating even if he didn't mean to be.

"We have a Grand Prix this weekend," Kyle said. "Could they be done by tomorrow morning?"

"Certainly," Jane said. She placed the two bridles on a blue hook. She took down two other bridles and handed them to Kyle. "Could you return these to Kelley and Talbot? It will save them a trip over here."

"Thank you, Ms. Jones. Good to see you, Sylvie."

Kyle head back to the jumper section of the barn.

The barn was built in four sections of twenty stalls each, connected by multiple tack rooms, feed rooms, grooming and wash stalls, barn office and large lounge area for the riders. The sections had naturally divided up among the various riding disciplines: dressage, hunters, eventers and jumpers. Scattered among the sections, there were a few endurance and competitive trail riders and one horse and owner that competed in carriage driving.

My horse Zeke and I were part of the hunter contingency. That being one of the quieter, less frantic areas of the barn, Jane's chair and complicated system of hooks and many tiered saddle racks resided in a small alcove of the common areas closest to the hunter aisle.

Before I left, I hugged Jane and wished her a pleasant weekend.

When I got back to the barn Monday afternoon, her chair was empty and the many hooks and saddle racks that surrounded it were devoid of tack.

"Where's Jane?" I asked no one in particular.

My voice, loud and alarmed, attracted several blank looks from people in the barn

Someone said, "She got killed."

My alarm turned to shock. Jane lived a half mile from the barn, in a cottage behind one of the large houses nearby, and walked to and from the barn, often in the early morning mist or after dark

"When?" I was barely able to speak. "Was she hit by a car?"

"Last night. She was strangled right here in the barn, in that chair she always sat in."

I knew the name of the girl who was telling me this, but did not care enough at the moment to remember it. I sat down on nearby tack trunk.

"Strangled? Murdered?"

"Yeah," the girl said. "The police have been all over the place."

"Someone got murdered here?" The question came from someone I didn't know and hadn't ever seen before. "Who was she?"

"I think she was just somebody's grandmother. She cleaned tack for the riders."

Just somebody's grandmother. I stared at the person who spoke so unfeelingly, but my eyes were full of tears and I couldn't focus on who it was. It occurred to me that in such a large facility, for as many of us as Jane was an adored friend, there were just as many who hardly noticed her. To many riders, who paid no attention to any of the staff, she was just another fixture.

Chelsea saw my distress and put her arm around me while I cried. She was one of the few people at the barn I was close to, mainly because neither of us had enough money to train and show constantly like most of the barn patrons.

I pulled myself together quickly. "I'm sorry," I said. "It's just so unexpected."

Chelsea patted my shoulder awkwardly before she went back to her horse.

Simply out of habit, I got Zeke's bridle (freshly cleaned and oiled) from where someone had placed it back on its hook. I grabbed my saddle and headed over to my horse's stall, where I tacked him up.

I walked Zeke through the whole barn toward the farthest door.

In the Jumper aisle Kyle was helping Blaire soak her horse's foot. Her gelding, Bob, had a puncture wound in the sole of a front hoof.

Debbie and William were hosting a casual recap with all the combined training riders of the event they'd competed in on Saturday. The dressage wing, always more quiet than the other sections of the barn even when really busy, was filled with people wrapping or unwrapping horses' legs with white polo wraps, a seemingly endless task.

Once outside I got on Zeke and we drifted out onto the trails. I was fortunate that he was a calm horse. I was so distracted that if he spooked at all, I would have no chance of staying in the saddle.

I thought about Jane and whether anyone would miss her the way I did. I wasn't the only person who relied on her for more than clean bridles and saddles. There was always someone talking to her, sometimes in small groups, but more often just one person, like a private counseling session.

What did other people talk to her about? Probably not news and politics. Maybe things like ideas for birthday gifts. Most likely problems; things regarding relationships, work or money.

I would have trusted her with anything I need to talk about, however difficult. She was the kind of person people just felt they could talk to. Could someone have told her something it was dangerous for her to know?

When I returned to the barn the police were there. I untacked Zeke and brushed him as the officers went through the barn seeking out people they hadn't spoken to yet. I was combing Zeke's tail when one of them got to me.

"Are you Ms. Sylvia Moore?" he asked.

"Yes, sir."

"We're investigating the death of Ms. Jane Jones."

I felt myself wanting to cry again.

"I'm sorry. I understand this is difficult," he said.

"I'm okay," I said. "She was the sweetest lady."

"Do you think anyone would have a motive for killing her?"

I told him about how so many people, like myself, looked to Jane as someone to confide in.

"Do you think she would use anything she heard to blackmail someone?" the officer asked.

"No. I couldn't imagine her doing that, but someone might have told her something and then decide they shouldn't have and wanted to keep her from repeating it."

"Have you noticed anyone that's been talking to her a lot lately? Or if she seemed upset after speaking with a particular person?"

"I go to school and work full time," I said. "I'm almost never here."

I guessed there was just as much chance that a maniac with no motive had just wandered in and strangled Jane for no reason at all. Would Jane have let a stranger get close enough to strangle her without raising some kind of alarm? Did that mean it was someone she trusted or was a least familiar with?

The detective asked how long I'd know her, where I went to school and where I'd been over the weekend, specifically Sunday night. I answered, wanting to be helpful, but knowing nothing I said had any real value.

I finished up with Zeke and put him back in his stall. Restlessly, I wandered through the barn. I ended up in the jumper aisle where Kyle and Blaine were again, or still, talking about Bob's hoof injury.

"It had to be a nail or piece of wire," Blaine said.

Kyle nodded. "We have two people on staff whose only job is to make sure that everything is maintained and repaired. I don't know how horses can be so self destructive in an environment we strive to keep safe for them. Like that huge cut on Jekyll's shoulder. How did he do that?"

Blaine and I didn't have the answer. It did seem like if there was the slightest possibility for a horse to get hurt, they did. For being such large, strong animals, they were incredibly delicate.

Blaine gave her horse a carrot and headed to her car, leaving Kyle and me alone.

"Kyle, did anyone here really know anything about Jane?" I asked.

Kyle looked sad and shook his head.

"It's amazing that she was a fixture here for the past few years and yet no one knew anything about her personally," he said. "She didn't have any family. Devon and I will arrange a funeral for her later this week at her church. There's a beautiful cemetery right next to it. Devon and Megan are going to pick out a plot there for her."

"Could it have been someone from here?"

Kyle scowled at my suggestion that someone involved with the farm might be responsible, and for a moment he looked as formidable as Devon.

"I really don't want people thinking this isn't a safe place or that one of the clients is a psychotic murderer," he said.

"Maybe she was targeted for a reason."

"Like what?"

"People were always talking to her. Maybe someone told her something they later regretted sharing. Maybe something unethical, incriminating or just humiliating. If she heard of or suspected someone doing anything unethical or criminal, she would expose it or report it to someone or at the very least confront the person about it."

Kyle looked thoughtful.

"If I ask some people I might find out who had been talking with Jane and about what," I offered.

"That's a good idea," Kyle said.

I suspected he thought the idea was as ridiculous as I did, but it helped just to think I was doing something.

"You had a Grand Prix this weekend," I said. "How did you do?"

Grand Prix was the highest level of Jumper competition, and there were several held in our area every year. Kyle and several other riders from the barn competed in the local ones, as a stepping stone to bigger things.

"I won, but only because Kelly's reins broke," he said modestly.

"Kelly's reins broke?" I repeated.

I remembered Jane handing Kelly's and Talbot's bridles to Kyle the previous Wednesday. There had been no brightly colored "needs repair" tags on them. It was hard to imagine that Jane would miss seeing a weakness in the reins, but it was possible. Sometimes even new leather broke and Kelly's bridle could have snagged on something in transit and been damaged.

"The reins broke right at the bit just before a big oxer," Kyle said "They almost crashed. It was scary."

"Do the rules or judges allow for that?" I asked. I didn't know much about jumper competition. "Couldn't she have another chance?"

"That depends on the circumstances, but Kelly was too shook up to ride after that. She would have beaten me, otherwise."

I thought he was being gracious. How many riders would admit they wouldn't have won, except for another's bad luck?

"Next time the bad luck might be mine," Kyle said, almost reading my thoughts.

"Did anyone else from here ride in it?"

"Eduardo and his horse, Lavor. They did really well; placed fifth."

"That is good," I said.

For Eduardo and Lavor it was. Eduardo had only been riding a few years and competing for one season, but Eduardo's riding and his horse's performance were improving fast. Soon they would be a serious challenge against the better riders.

"Congratulate Eduardo for me. Did Talbot not ride?" I asked.

"No. He was supposed to, but Jekyll got that shoulder laceration Friday afternoon."

"Who found Jane?" I asked Kyle. "Was anyone here when she was killed?"

"Kelly found her. It was early Sunday evening, so we didn't think anyone was here. Billy and I had loaded the horses to bring them home while the riders were packing up their stuff. We were unloading horses off the trailer when Kelly got here and she went straight over to Jane to ask her about the reins. It must have happened just before we got back."

"Was it possible the murderer was still here?" I asked.

"Who knows?" Kyle lowered his voice. "It's good that Kelly didn't get there a few minutes sooner."

"She could have saved Jane!"

"Sylvie, Kelly could have gotten killed, too. A person who kills for whatever reason, doesn't hesitate to kill again to keep from being found out."

That made me shiver. At the same time I thought of Kelly going in search of Jane while being furious about her bridle.

Kelly wouldn't do that, I thought. I didn't know her that well, but had the impression she was as philosophical as Kyle. New leather can break, I told myself again. Damage can happen in the mad scramble to get horses and riders and all their gear to a show.

I left Kyle and walked distractedly back to the hunter aisle.

I didn't know where to start. Everyone had already been questioned by the police. Those who were close to Jane would be upset and not want to talk about her. Those who weren't close to Jane wouldn't care and wouldn't want to talk about her.

I came across Heidi and her younger sister, Elsa, two of my favorite kids at the barn. The girls were friendly, smart and more mature than their ages of ten and eight. They were the antithesis of children who adults thought never paid attention to anything that didn't concern them directly; or children who wouldn't understand certain things about adult life without it being explained to them.

"Hi, guys," I said. "We're you here yesterday?"

I tried to sound as normal as possible, but I knew I wasn't completely successful. Being who they were, the girls noticed. Only Heidi, the older one, seemed to know why. Heidi watched me anxiously and I determined that Elsa didn't know about Jane. I tried to convey to Heidi without speaking that I wouldn't mention it.

"We were here for a lesson with Jamie," Heidi said. "But we had to leave by four because our brother had a soccer game."

Ordinarily it amused me that kids always thought they were being cheated if they didn't get to stay at the barn until bed time. In this instance, I was glad they hadn't still been here while there was a killer lurking in the barn. At the same time, I couldn't help feeling that if someone had been here, Jane might not have been murdered.

"Who was around the barn?" I asked.

Heidi didn't respond, but Elsa, who liked to talk, was happy to have an audience.

"Most of the eventers were off because they had that thing Saturday," she said. "On Sunday they let the horses rest, so none of them were here except Rick. Rick only came by for a minute. He had the flu; he looked awful."

"A lot of the dressage riders were here," Heidi said. "They had a clinic yesterday afternoon with Natasha and were still putting their horses away. The Jumper people were all gone to the Grand Prix and most of the hunter riders were gone by afternoon."

"Was anyone here with Jane?" I asked.

Heidi and I watched Elsa carefully, but Elsa wasn't suspicious about my question. While we talked, Elsa concentrated on removing the bit from her pony's bridle and replacing it with a new one, a sometimes difficult process.

"Just Jamie, who wanted to ask Jane to oil her bridle next week while she's at her sister's wedding. Tory will be exercising Jamie's horse while she's gone and Tory doesn't look after her tack very well." Elsa said this casually, as if she didn't realize she was—or didn't mean to be—insulting Tory's horsemanship practices.

"Have you noticed if anyone has been talking to Jane a lot lately?"

"I hadn't noticed," Heidi said.

Elsa glanced at me and then at Heidi, but we both managed to look relaxed.

"Someone's always talking to Jane, every day. Molly has been, because Lisa's been so mean to her." Elsa was glad to share her knowledge with someone. "Carrie talked with Jane for awhile, 'cause she was worried about her horse. Carrie's mare is the jumper who colicked twice this month."

Heidi and I listened as Elsa went on with her observations.

"Dudley asked Jane about the frayed stitching on his saddle because he couldn't find it and she showed him where it was so he could get it fixed. And Sophie talked to her a bunch last week about her divorce."

Sophie talked long and loudly about her divorce to everyone, including the horses and the barn cats. It was the comment about Carrie's horse colicking that got my attention.

"Didn't Molly's horse colic not long ago?" I asked.

"Yes," Heidi said. "I remember because they missed that Grand Prix in June and she'd been so excited about it, since she and her horse did so well at the one in April. She thought they had a chance to win."

"That was the same time one of the event horses colicked and two of the dressage horses and one lesson pony," Elsa added. "I thought they blamed it on a bad batch of feed or some kind of undetected mold in the hay."

Colic was another way horses were delicate. The term colic in a horse referred to any kind of intestinal pain. It could be as minor as a mild cramp or a fatal twist or knot in the intestine. It was often hard to tell how serious it was, but since severe colic could result in death within hours, every case was dealt with as potentially life threatening.

"Thanks guys," I said, and went in search of Kyle.

"Can I speak to you alone," I asked, when I found him. "I think I have some relevant information."

"Sure. Meet me in the barn office at feeding time, when everyone's gone," he said.

He looked concerned. He certainly wouldn't be happy if I had something that might point to someone among his staff or clients being a murderer.

I cleaned my saddle while I waited until feeding was done. The movement seemed to relax the muscles in my hands and lessen the pain in my wrists.

Devon wandered by with his fiancé Megan and I smiled at them. Devon made me uncomfortable, but Megan was friendly and reminded me of Kyle.

Kyle waved to me and we went into the barn office. It was a large room, with a desk, a small sofa and an impressive trophy case, displaying awards gathered by Devon and Kyle. There were saddles on racks in the corner and bridles hanging on the wall next to the door.

Kyle sat behind the desk and I perched on the couch next to the door, facing him. I didn't know how to explain what I had come up with.

"This may sound absurd," I said. "But I'll tell you what I think and you can give me your opinion. It occurred to me when I remembered those horses colicking several weeks ago."

Kyle grimaced. Horses colicked for almost any reason; stress, too much or too little exercise, a change in food or even a change in the weather. All horse owners understood it could be caused by a number of things or sometimes nothing at all.

However, the group of cases I mentioned to had been somehow attributed to a problem with the feed or hay and that reflected badly on the farm management

"I put Molly's horse's colic together with the incidents of Blaine's horse's punctured foot, Jekyll's slashed shoulder, and Kelly's broken bridle. Other areas of the barn have their share of catastrophes, but most things have only affected the Jumpers that compete at the Grand Prix level.

"I thought about the recent show performance of the Grand Prix horses and it occurred to me that something has happened to everyone's horses out of competition recently—except Eduardo's horse, Lavor. I hate to think that someone we know is hurting horses, but if it were a person who's around all the time, they would have plenty of opportunities."

"You think someone—Eduardo—is deliberately keeping horses from competing?" Kyle asked.

"Or hurting their chances to win," I said. "You saw Kelly's bridle when Jane handed it to you after cleaning last week. There was nothing wrong with it. Eduardo could have sabotaged Kelly's reins before the Grand Prix. He would have had plenty of opportunity. You know how chaotic it is getting the horses and everything to a show."

Kyle said, "Nothing's happened to put my horse out of competition."

"Eduardo wouldn't do that to you. He worships you."

As I said this I realized the implication of Kyle's remark. I had difficulty accepting that Kyle might have done those things. Which could mean he then killed Jane, because if Kelly asked her about the bridle, Jane's quick mind might have made her suspicious. These thoughts made me slow to react to my situation.

Kyle was out of his chair and around the desk before I moved. The office door was right next to the couch, but as I stood up Kyle put himself between me and the door.

I didn't see the bridle he'd taken off the wall until he had looped the reins over my head.   Devon and Megan had to still be out in the barn somewhere, but the barn was a big place. I managed one really loud scream before Kyle yanked the reins tightly around my throat.

I tried to pull away, but I couldn't move. Kyle remained where he was in front of the door. When the door was suddenly kicked open, it hit Kyle solidly enough to slam him back into the wall. The pain of the reins twisted around my neck increased as he tried to use the bridle and my weight to keep his balance, but he only managed to pull me down to the floor with him.

The pressure let up when Devon lifted Kyle half off the floor and hit him hard enough to knock him out. As Devon untangled me from the bridle I only remained conscious long enough to hear Megan pick up the phone and press three numbers.


I was treated and released from the ER the same night, but couldn't speak well enough to give the police a statement until the next day.  I was recovered enough the day after that to attend the service for Jane, which was beautiful.

Devon invited all the farm clients to a meeting at the barn where he explained everything as the police had reported it. He apologized to the Grand Prix riders for the damage Kyle had done and offered reimbursement for vet bills and even the repair bill for Kelly's bridle.

There were enough people not involved with the whole situation and who hadn't been close to Jane personally, that more than one person asked, "Who's going to clean my bridle?"

I was surprised to hear myself answer, "I will."

"Good. When you clean you own bridle and saddle they always look great."

Before I left the barn, I had a growing list of instructions and a collection of tack to be cleaned that I labeled and organized on Jane's hooks.

Even through the loss of her presence and wisdom, Jane had given me the gift of a new and more favorable livelihood.

Made in the USA
Columbia, SC
17 April 2023